Sir Fabian was offering her carte blanche...

He raked her face and body with a long, hatefully approving glance. "Well? How does my proposition strike you? Are you at all interested?"

She had allowed him to speak without interruption, but now she exploded.

"No, I am *not* interested, sir. On the contrary, I am insulted to the core by your 'proposition.' I would rather beg on the streets than live under the protection of a man with so little breeding."

"A vixen like you wouldn't know a man of breeding if she met one," snarled Sir Fabian, his face flushed an angry red. "I think that I'll just have to give you a lesson in how to speak to your betters."

He advanced on her purposefully, and Dorinda found herself cornered near the fireplace. Sir Fabian paused several feet away from her, his lips curved in an ugly grin. "I take back my offer, my girl, but before I leave I'm going to show you what you'll be missing..."

DORINDA

Diana Delmore

WARNER BOOKS

A Warner Communications Company

Warner Books, Inc.
75 Rockefeller Plaza
New York, N.Y. 10019

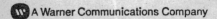 A Warner Communications Company

Printed in the United States of America

First Printing: September, 1985

10 9 8 7 6 5 4 3 2 1

Chapter I

"But I thought you understood, Miss Hayle, that your stepfather's income ended with his death."

The elderly lawyer lifted an eyebrow in mild surprise as he gazed at the quiet, dark girl sitting across the desk from him. Dorinda Hayle bit her lip for she thought that she detected a note of reproach in Mr. Stowe's voice, almost as if she had questioned his handling of her stepfather's financial affairs.

"Yes, of course. I knew Lord Roger's allowance ceased with his death last November, but I came to see you today because I thought—I hoped—that Lady Torrington might have notified you that she planned to make some provision for my mother."

Mr. Stowe shook his head regretfully. "No, I've received no word at all from Lady Torrington in the past two months, except for a brief note thanking me for sending her the news of her son's death. I must confess that I was a little surprised when she did not come here to Brighton at the time of the funeral, or even send a family representative, but . . . ah, well, it's not for me to judge her ladyship's conduct." He cleared his throat. "It's unfortunate that your mother has no income of her own, and that because of Lord Roger's . . . ah, way of life . . . he could not put anything aside for her future, but, Miss Hayle, I can give you no hope at all that Lady Torrington will provide for Lady Roger. You are quite aware, I'm sure, that her ladyship disapproved violently of her son's marriage."

"Oh, yes. I'm well aware that Lord Roger Wingate put himself outside the family pale when he married my mother, who was not only an actress but who was encumbered with an illegitimate child," said Dorinda, a spot of color high on each of her cheeks. "But one would think that almost twenty years of respectable married life would count for something. I'm sorry, Mr. Stowe. I have no right to burden you with my problems."

"No, no. Pray don't apologize. If I could be of any help . . . perhaps a small personal loan, just to tide you over your immediate difficulties. . . ."

Dorinda's color heightened, but she said quite composedly, "Thank you for your kind thought, but I couldn't accept a loan, Mr. Stowe. Mama and I can manage very well for the present, and I will simply have to look for some kind of employment."

Nonetheless, Dorinda felt far from composed as she left the lawyer's office and stepped out into the busy traffic of North Street, where the London stagecoach was just departing from in front of the Castle Inn. As she felt a chill breeze from off the sea, she shivered, drawing her collar closer around her throat, and glanced at the small watch attached to the bodice of her pelisse. It was too early to meet Mrs. Vane, the vicar's wife, who had driven her to Brighton, so she began to stroll aimlessly, filling in time, hardly noticing her surroundings as her thoughts reverted to her mother's pressing financial problems.

It had been a forlorn hope, this visit to Mr. Stowe. For the past eighteen years, Lord Roger Wingate had been as good as dead to Lady Torrington and the rest of his family. Even before his marriage, Lord Roger, the younger son of the Fifth Marquess of Torrington, had been the family black sheep—a drunkard, a gambler, a wencher—but his union with Charlotte Hayle, a minor member of a provincial acting company, had caused the Wingates to wash their collective hands of him. In return for a small yearly allowance of three hundred pounds, Lord Roger had agreed to refrain from associating with any of his relatives, and to go into exile in a small house leased for him by his mother in a tiny village about five miles from Brighton.

Only five years old when her mother had married Lord Roger, Dorinda had only the haziest memories of her first years in Brighton. Her stepfather seemed to have been away from home rather more often than not, and his wife had spent much of her time reclining on a chaise longue, gently wiping away the tears occasioned by her husband's neglect. For, in the beginning, Lord Roger had been able to continue his usual way of life, though on a limited scale; he was a regular patron of the racecourse in Brighton, and he could also enjoy the company of those of his old cronies who flocked to lodgings in Brighton as the resort town became increasingly popular under the patronage of the young Prince of Wales. But for the last ten years of his life, plagued by growing health problems brought on by his lifelong alcoholism and by attacks of the Wingate family curse, gout, Lord Roger had been a reluctantly reformed rake. Beginning in her middle teens, his stepdaughter had assumed charge of the household from her erratic and butterflylike mother, and in her quietly capable way had forced Lord Roger into involuntary sobriety. Rarely ventur-

ing beyond the confines of the tiny village, Lord Roger, in
the twilight of his life, found himself living a constricted
existence, enlivened only by visits and informal dinners with
the vicar, the local doctor, and the squire, Mr. Cowleigh.

Dorinda had been fond of her stepfather, and he of her,
and today, as she roamed the streets of Brighton, she caught
herself wondering with a little pang of amused solicitude if
Lord Roger might have died of acute boredom. Perhaps he
would have died happier—if considerably sooner—with a
bottle of port at one elbow and a pack of playing cards at the
other.

Dorinda's smile faded as her chronic financial worries
resurfaced. She had managed to save a little money from
the household accounts over the past few months, and the
lease of the house had fortunately been renewed for another
year shortly before Lord Roger's death. There were some
retrenchments that she could make, but eventually her little
hoard of money would run out. Before that happened she
would have to find some form of employment, but that was
far easier said than done. Dorinda felt herself to be well
educated—Lord Roger had sent her to a good if minor
boarding school—yet the only positions open to a gentlewoman were those of governess or companion. Not only were
both these professions poorly paid, but Dorinda was apprehensive about her chances of obtaining a post in view of her
dubious family background. How many employers would
willingly engage a governess or a companion who was the
daughter of an actress and herself illegitimate? Probably
not many, judging by a boarding-school memory that still
rankled: Dorinda had been invited to a classmate's home for
a much anticipated visit, only to have the invitation
rescinded when the classmate's mother learned of Dorinda's
parentage.

Dorinda looked up to find that she had wandered off
North Street into a narrow tree-lined lane called Poplar

Place. She paused in front of a dress shop to gaze into the tiny, square-paned windows at a French fashion that had caught her eye: an evening dress of diaphanous net over a robe of shimmering gold lamé with a deep flounce of blond lace. Displayed beside the evening fashion was a day dress of blue silk with a deep ruff and Spanish trimmings on the long tight sleeves. Momentary visions of herself in these elegant creations faded into wistfulness; in Eastfield village not even the squire's wife would have the occasion to wear such dresses. Dorinda was about to turn away when a bold thought struck her. Hesitating for a nervous instant, she forced herself to open the door and walk into the shop, where a French-looking lady was pointing out the beauties of an evening costume, an emerald satin gown with a practically nonexistent neckline, to a young man and his female companion.

Standing quietly by the door, Dorinda gazed with considerable interest at the young man, who appeared to be a prime example of the dandy set so much admired by Martin Cowleigh, the squire's son. But poor Martin's attempts to dress in the height of fashion paled beside the splendor of this young Pink of the Ton, who wore a many-caped full-length box coat of white drab embellished with an enormous bouquet of flowers in the buttonhole, and whose cravat was so high that it seemed to be pushing his ears out of position. The lady accompanying him wore a velvet pelisse in an overpowering shade of purple and a matching hat topped by enormous ostrich plumes dyed a bright yellow.

"Oh, Willyum, 'ow lov'ly," cooed the lady. "Can I 'ave it, lovey? Please? And 'ow about the witzchoura mantle with the sable collar?"

"Well, a hundred guineas seems a bit dear . . . oh, very well, Rosie, go along and try it on for size," said William indulgently, and it dawned on the rather scandalized Dorinda that she was seeing, close up, that whispered-about feature of fashionable society known as the "ladybird," the "high flyer," the "dressy bit of muslin."

Before accompanying her customer into the fitting room, the proprietress turned her attention to Dorinda, advancing toward her with a welcoming smile that faded as she observed Dorinda's modest pelisse of black merino and her simple bonnet.

"Yes?" said the woman coolly. "May I help you?"

"I don't wish to buy anything, madame," Dorinda said hastily. "But ... I was wondering ... if by chance you would have any need for a shop assistant?"

Madame favored her with a long, critically examining glance that left Dorinda feeling very nervous. "As it happens, I've been considering engaging someone to replace my present assistant who has just left to be married," replied the woman at last. "You seem quite well-spoken and presentable, mademoiselle. Yes, you just might do. Wait here for me until I've finished with my customer."

As Madame disappeared into the fitting room, Dorinda felt a small surge of hope. She was sure that the dress shop position would not pay very much, and Madame did not strike her as a particularly kindly employer, but even the slenderest of wages would be helpful at this point. Working here would at least give her breathing room until she could find something more suitable.

"So you're thinkin' of takin' a position here, are you, m'love? A cloth-headed thing to do, if you ask me. A prime article like yourself could do much better elsewhere, I assure you."

Dorinda looked up in affronted surprise to find the young dandy smiling down at her. "You have the advantage of me, sir," she said frigidly. "I don't believe that I know you."

The dandy's smile faded slightly. "Devilish high in the instep, ain't you, m'girl? I may not be awake on every suit, but you can't bamboozle me into thinking that you're a lady of quality. Not when you're applying to work in a dress shop. What kind of a flat do you take me for?" His manner growing in confidence, he moved closer to Dorinda, putting one hand on her shoulder and the other under her chin. "Come now, m'girl, let's get to know each other a little better. What about a little kiss to start?"

Her eyes blazing, Dorinda thrust both hands against his chest in a determined shove that sent him reeling across the floor.

" 'Ere now! Willyum! Whatcher doing there?"

Catching his balance, William turned to face his irate ladylove. "Now, Rosie . . . the young lady and I were just havin' a little chat." He smiled ingratiatingly. "By George, if that dress don't beat the Dutch. I never saw you dressed so becomingly."

While Rosie, considerably mollified, was pirouetting in the emerald satin gown before the enthusiastic William, Madame stalked over to Dorinda.

"I've changed my mind, mademoiselle. I won't be needing your services."

"But, madame, if you'd just let me explain. . . ."

Casting a quick look behind her to see if Rosie and William were still occupied with each other, the proprietress said in a low voice, "I understand perfectly, and I'm not accusing you of any misconduct. But you are just too pretty a girl, my dear. I cannot take the risk of having you offend any of my female customers . . . if you see what I mean."

Dorinda did see—very clearly. She thanked Madame and left the shop, feeling even more depressed than when she had entered it. She returned to steep, crowded North Street and walked down to the New Road and thence to the grounds of the Marine Pavilion and the red brick pavement of the Steyne, so refreshing in summer with its neatly laid out gardens. She took up a position to wait for the vicar's wife in front of the low wall separating the entrance of the

Pavilion from the street. She had, of course, seen this product of the regent's building enthusiasm many times, but she experienced a fresh feeling of astonishment as she gazed upon the riot of green-roofed domes and cupolas and minarets, and at the cones in Greek, Chinese, Moorish, and Russian styles—all crowning the roof of the vast building. Someone had once told her that the regent's fertile brain had conceived the vaguely Oriental design of the structure many years ago when a friend had sent him a present of some Chinese wallpaper.

"Here I am at last, my dear. I fear that I'm a little late."

Beginning to feel quite chilled from her wait, Dorinda climbed with relief into the vicarage carriage which had just pulled up beside her. After the coachman had closed the door, Dorinda turned to Mrs. Vane with a smile, saying, "Please don't apologize. I haven't been waiting very long, and in any case I'm just so grateful for the ride into town. Were you able to find all the things that you were looking for?"

"Oh, yes. Even to the cherry ribbon to match the little dress I'm having made for my granddaughter." Stout, middle-aged, and warm-hearted, Mrs. Vane had always had a soft spot in her heart for Dorinda. "How about your morning?"

"Not very fruitful, I'm afraid. Mr. Stowe could offer me no encouragement about a possible allowance for Mama."

"I see." Mrs. Vane was well acquainted with Dorinda's family financial problems, but she was not a pry or a gossip, nor was she one to offer false encouragement. "I wish that I could think of something helpful, my dear."

"Thank you, Mrs. Vane, but I'm sure something will turn up. Please don't worry about me and Mama," said Dorinda, voicing an optimism she did not feel. She lapsed into a thoughtful silence that the sympathetic Mrs. Vane did not attempt to interrupt as they drove north out of Brighton through the low rolling hill country of the South Downs for about five miles, finally turning into the narrow lane that led to the tiny village of Eastfield, which consisted only of a church, a parsonage, several small houses and shops, and the larger, more imposing home of the squire, Mr. Cowleigh.

At the entrance to the village they were hailed by Martin Cowleigh, the squire's son, who dismounted from his horse and opened the door of the carriage. "Good day, Mrs. Vane, Dorinda," he said with a delighted smile that lit up his bright blue eyes and ingenuous young face. "I was afraid I would miss saying good-bye to you. I leave for Oxford this afternoon, you know."

"Yes, I did know. I hope that you have a safe and pleasant journey, Martin," said Mrs. Vane, to which Dorinda added a mischievous, "Be sure to keep your nose glued to your books." He laughed good-naturedly and, after a few minutes of conversation directed rather more to Dorinda than to the vicar's wife, took his leave.

"I daresay the squire and his wife will be relieved to see Martin returning to Oxford," said Mrs. Vane. "Mrs. Cowleigh was remarking to me just the other day that Martin seemed to have a great deal of idle time on his hands."

Dorinda quite understood that Mrs. Vane's rather aimless comment was meant as an oblique warning, and she did not really resent it. For the past year she and, indeed, most of the village had become increasingly aware that Martin had lost his heart to her. Dorinda felt nothing but friendship for Martin, whom she considered—he was almost three years younger than herself—as little more than an overgrown boy. But she knew perfectly well that the match would have been totally unsuitable even if she had cared for Martin and their ages had been more compatible. Mr. and Mrs. Cowleigh naturally aimed higher for their only son than a girl with flawed parentage and a complete absence of fortune, and

Martin's attendance on Dorinda obviously worried them.
She did wonder sometimes, however, why the squire and his
wife did not place a greater reliance on Dorinda's own
common sense.

Dropped by Mrs. Vane at her front gate, Dorinda went up
the walk of the "cottage" that had been her home for
eighteen years. It was a small house, bisected by a narrow
corridor that led directly from the front entrance to the little
garden behind. On each side of the entrance there was a
small sitting room, one of which had been used by Lord
Roger as his study, and upstairs there were four tiny bed-
rooms and a garret.

As Dorinda entered the cottage, her mother called out to
her from the sitting room. Charlotte Wingate, Lady Roger
Wingate as she loved to be known, was half sitting, half
reclining on a sofa, a bit of embroidery work drooping from
her fingers. She was still a very attractive woman, with a
graceful, slender figure, a winsome unlined face, and fluffy
dark blond curls, and she looked far younger than her
years—the early forties. Her youthful appearance reflected
her placid, rather childlike personality and her comfortable
philosophy that most problems in life could be trusted to
solve themselves. As Dorinda gazed at her mother, who was
wearing a particularly fetching lace cap, she reflected that
most people who met Charlotte would find it difficult to
credit her notoriety. To the uninitiated, Charlotte would
appear to be simply a very pretty, sweet, soft-spoken gentlewoman, a trifle faded, perhaps, but not in the least a moral
reprobate. And, indeed, Dorinda had always thought this
appraisal closer to the mark than her mother's reputation
would suggest. Charlotte Hayle's father had been a respectable small-town solicitor, and she had received a perfectly
adequate education. When she had run away to join a band
of strolling actors her parents had been shocked into dis-

owning her as thoroughly as, a few years later, the Wingate family had washed their hands of Lord Roger.

"There you are, darling. Did you enjoy your little jaunt to Brighton?" said Charlotte amiably, laying aside her embroidery, which in truth she seldom actually worked upon. "So kind of the vicar's wife to take you with her. I think that you should go more often."

"As you well know, Mama, I went into Brighton to see Mr. Stowe," replied Dorinda rather impatiently. "And I'm sorry to be obliged to tell you that there can be no question of renewing Papa's allowance."

Charlotte was unruffled. "Don't look so concerned, dearest. I feel sure that Lady Torrington will eventually see her duty. Well, I mean she can't really be such a monster— though of course I never actually met her—as to allow her granddaughter to be in want."

"Stepgranddaughter. A very different relationship—or lack of one."

"But, darling, it's very much the same thing, don't you think?" replied Charlotte vaguely. "Oh, I must tell you: Martin Cowleigh called this morning while you were gone . . . such a nice young man. Do you know, I really think that he might offer for you, Dorinda, if you gave him the slightest encouragement."

About to toss her mother an exasperated denial, Dorinda shrugged. It was useless to expect Charlotte to change her easygoing ways. Instead Dorinda said, "Look, Mama, I must talk to you about money. Mrs. Vane told me this morning that you were thinking of replacing the carpet and the window hangings in the sitting room."

"Indeed I am. This room is beginning to look disgracefully shabby."

"We can't afford to replace so much as the fringe on the carpet. In fact, in view of what Mr. Stowe told me today, we're going to have to cut down on every expense that we can."

"But how can we economize any further?" protested Charlotte. "We've already given up the houseman and sold the carriage. Soon we'll be living like common laborers."

"It may well come to that, Mama," said Dorinda grimly. "Tomorrow I'm going to dismiss the gardener and the cook, and we may not even be able to keep Elspeth."

At that moment Elspeth, the little maid of all work, entered the room to announce that a gentleman had called to see Lady Roger. "Name of Desmond Barry, my lady."

"Who could it be, Mama? We don't know any Barrys."

Charlotte wrinkled her forehead. "Desmond Barry? Could it possibly be? . . . Show Mr. Barry in, Elspeth."

The tall, slender man who followed the maidservant into the room appeared to be in his early thirties. He had dark red hair, lively blue eyes, and a pleasantly handsome face. To Dorinda, accustomed to Lord Roger's conservative elegance, the newcomer's attire—bright blue coat, yellow pantaloons, and red waistcoat—seemed a trifle garish. His tasseled cane was clearly no mere fashion accessory; though he walked slowly and used the cane skillfully, he could not quite conceal a pronounced limp.

Charlotte rose to meet her guest. Extending her hand, she said, "How do you do, Mr. Barry. I am Lady Roger Wingate."

Bowing gracefully despite his use of the cane, Mr. Barry kissed Charlotte's hand with a flourish. "Beautiful as ever, I swear, Lady Roger. You look exactly the same as you did the last time I saw you; you played Edwina to my father's Percy."

Clapping her hands in childlike delight, Charlotte exclaimed, "Why, that was ages ago. Let me see now . . . it must have been about 1793, just before I married Lord Roger. And so you are John Barry's son. I don't understand how you can remember me at all. You were just a little boy when I left your father's company to get married."

Desmond Barry laughed. "Thank you for the compliment, Lady Roger, but I was almost grown-up in 1793. I was fourteen—no, fifteen—years old. I'm getting to be an old man, alas!" Turning to Dorinda, he said with an easy smile, "You must be Lady Roger's daughter. You're—now, wait a moment, it's coming to me—you're Dorinda. What a lovely name, and how lovely your mother looked when she played the part! You know, of course, that she named you after her role in *The Beaux' Stratagem*."

"Of course she knows," beamed Charlotte. "I only wish that Dorinda could have seen me in the role. It was quite the best part that I ever had . . . and John Barry was so kind. Once I joined the company, he never gave the role to anyone else. My dear Desmond, how is your father?"

"Dead these ten years, I regret to say. I took over the company when he died, of course, but it's not the same. Father was twice the actor that I will ever be."

"I'm so sorry to hear that," said Charlotte, tears welling into her soft eyes.

"You're playing an engagement in Brighton, are you, Mr. Barry?" asked Dorinda.

"Yes, we just arrived yesterday. This is a new area for us. We've been playing the northern circuits for many years. I had a vague recollection that you had retired somewhere near here, Lady Roger, and when I inquired after you I was told that his lordship had died several months ago. So I've come to offer my belated condolences."

Charlotte pressed his hand. "How kind. I'm *so* pleased to see you. But where are my manners? Do come over here and sit down with me on the sofa. You'll have a glass of wine? Dorinda, my dear, please ring for Elspeth. And now, Desmond, tell me all about yourself. Are you still playing only in the provinces? I remember so well how your father used to speak of getting a license for a London theatre."

"Oh, that." Desmond Barry grimaced. "Yes, I managed to get a license several years ago for a small theatre on 'Surreyside,' but I had to give it up. It's very difficult, you know, for the 'summer' theatres to make a success of it. They can play only from early in June to mid-September, and of course they can't perform straight drama at all."

"Summer theatres?" asked Dorinda curiously, as she brought Desmond a glass of wine.

"Thank you." Desmond smiled, lifting his glass to her. "Yes, the two Patent or Winter Theatres—at Drury Lane and Covent Garden—are the only ones permitted, under a Royal Patent going back to the reign of Charles II, to remain open during the winter months and to play legitimate drama." He chuckled. "Sometimes the minor or summer theatres get around the rules by changing the title of a play, inserting a few songs and dances and calling the result a 'burletta.' For instance, *Othello* became *The Venetian Moor*. The Lord Chamberlain is inclined to avert his eyes if a production has enough singing and dancing in it!"

As Dorinda tried rather bemusedly to imagine a dancing Othello, her mother said sympathetically, "I'm so sorry that your London venture didn't succeed, Desmond. Will you stay with provincial touring, then?"

Desmond shook his head. "Not if I can help it, Lady Roger. There's no doubt that the real money and recognition come from working in the Patent Theatres." He pointed to his cane. "If I hadn't come a cropper with my right leg, London is where I should be right now. I was engaged two seasons ago by Kemble at Covent Garden. Oh, no big roles. A few lines as Almagro in *Pizarro*. A good deal of spear carrying. But it was a start, and meanwhile Jack Wright of my touring company could take my place as manager in the provinces. I landed my first really good role, as Tybalt in

Romeo and Juliet, at the beginning of last season. Then, as my cursed luck would have it, I broke my leg during my first sword fight with Mercutio. I returned to my own company to wait for the bone to heal, and I hope to go back to Covent Garden within a few more weeks."

Desmond broke off, smiting his forehead in mock contrition. "But pray excuse me, Lady Roger. Here I come to visit an old friend and then spend all my time talking about my own affairs." He glanced around the room. "This seems like a snug little property. Will you and Miss Wingate stay on here?"

"My name is Hayle, Mr. Barry," Dorinda reminded him. "Lord Roger was my stepfather. Our plans are still rather indefinite."

"Well, of course we should love to stay on here, Desmond," said Charlotte wistfully. "It *is* a dear, comfortable little house, and we have such good friends here, the vicar and his wife, Dr. Kenton, Squire Cowleigh and his family, everyone most kind and obliging. But darling Dorinda tells me that we may not be able to keep the house. My husband had only a life allowance from his family, you know. But there, I keep assuring her that something will turn up, and so it will."

Desmond whistled. "You mean Lord Roger was in Dun territory? Somehow I thought . . . well, you'd expect the son of a marquess to come into the world rich as a nabob, but then he was a younger son, wasn't he? Surely the Wingates won't allow you to go fast aground."

Dorinda frowned in quick annoyance at the lack of gentility displayed by both her companions in discussing her mother's financial problems. Desmond, for all that he had been acquainted with Charlotte in the past, had not seen her for many years. He could not be considered a close friend, and he was a complete stranger to Dorinda. Nonetheless Dorinda relaxed, shrugging inwardly. Probably both Charlotte and Desmond were only reflecting their actors' background. No doubt everyone in the company knew to a shilling what the other players were receiving in salary, and even the most prominent actors counted on benefit performances to augment their incomes.

"Yes, I fear that we're not too plump in the pocket at the moment, Mr. Barry," she said now, trying for a light touch, "but Mama is quite right, something will turn up. I've been thinking of looking for employment."

Desmond again grated on her sensibilities by his frank appraisal of her situation. "Employment? Lombard Street to a China orange, the only positions open to you are those of governess or of companion to some old lady. I certainly can't see you as a shopgirl," he remarked skeptically, lifting his eyebrow as Dorinda flushed in memory of her encounter with "Willyum" in Madame's dress shop.

Desmond looked at Dorinda with a calculating eye. He saw a rather tall, slender, graceful girl of twenty three, with a mass of dark wavy hair, large brown eyes, a straight little nose and well-formed mouth, and a creamy complexion. "Have you ever thought of going on the stage?" he asked abruptly. "From the looks of you, you might do breeches parts divinely. You certainly have the figure for it. Have you ever done any amateur theatricals?"

"No, I have not," said Dorinda frigidly. "I have no talent for the theatre at all, and even if I did, I couldn't consider a stage career."

"But it might be the very thing, darling," spoke up Charlotte excitedly. "Now, why didn't I ever think of that? A successful stage career for you would solve all our problems. Well, not acting perhaps, but you have a beautiful voice. Do sing for Desmond that little song I like so much, the one you played at the vicarage last week."

Dorinda's first impulse was to refuse to sing, but at length she sat down at the pianoforte, saying, "Very well, Mama,

Mr. Barry will see just how prejudiced your opinions are." She was soon caught up, despite herself, in playing and singing, in her clear light soprano, the lovely Elizabethan air, "All in a Garden Green".

His face beaming, Desmond came up to Dorinda at the pianoforte. "Lady Roger has excellent taste. You have a superlative voice, Miss Hayle. You'll be doing me a service, and yourself, too, if you accept a role in a new play that I'm about to mount at the theatre in the New Road in Brighton. A musical version of *The Lady of the Lake*. My leading actress, Cassandra Bell, has just come down with a putrid throat, and I'd be bamming you if I told you that she had much of a voice to begin with."

Dorinda recoiled. "No, no. I couldn't possibly appear in your play. For that matter, I can't conceive of a musical version of *The Lady of the Lake*. I've read Mr. Scott's poem, and it has a very serious story."

"Oh, well, there's nothing to that. You can turn any play or poem into a burletta if you just add some incidental music and at least five songs to every act, and you'll have no trouble putting it on the boards even in London. The public is bored with heavy tragedy, you know. They like a good melodrama, or a story with music and dancing and a little high comedy. I'll tell you what, Miss Hayle: If you play the part of Ellen in my *Lady of the Lake*, I'll wager that it will do even better than the Siddons version of last season."

"I'm sure that I wish your play every success, but it must be without me. Under no circumstances would I appear on the stage," said Dorinda firmly, cringing at the very thought of continuing into the second generation the odium that had always been attached to Charlotte's theatrical career.

Chapter II

Standing in the wings, Dorinda watched with considerable amusement an energetic run-through of a new *Chinese Harlequinade* that Desmond was putting into the evening's bill, filched, he had admitted quite cheerfully, from a presentation of *The Mandarin* at Sadler's Wells in 1788—"Except that our version, of course is, much better!" On joining Desmond's company a scant two weeks previously, Dorinda had been astonished at the length of the nightly program, which began at six-thirty and ended at midnight. Audiences demanded their money's worth, Desmond had told her, and so, in addition to the main piece, the program had to include pantomime, assorted singing and dancing, and specialty acts such as rope dancing, tightrope walking, and strong man exhibitions.

After the pantomime rehearsal, Desmond walked out on the stage calling, "Felton, Adams, get along up here. I'd like to give you a few pointers about your third-act duelling scene. I thought last night that you were getting just a bit lackadaisical."

As Dorinda watched the two actors go through their paces as the broadswordsmen Roderick and Fitz-James, she murmured to Jack Wright, the assistant manager, who was standing beside her, "It's difficult to see how they could be any more realistic. They're such skilled fencers."

Jack Wright smiled. "Ah, but you've never seen Desmond in a duelling scene. If it weren't for his game leg— Well, Felton's good enough in the part, but it's Desmond who should be playing Roderick, Miss Conroy."

Dorinda blinked at the use of her stage name, with which she still felt totally unfamiliar. She had dug in her heels at Desmond's persuasions that she accept a role in his new play, and had given in, most unwillingly, only after he had assured her that the assumed name of Rachel Conroy and a blond wig would conceal her identity on stage from any friends or acquaintances who might be in the audience, and that her real name would be withheld even from her fellow cast members.

"Desmond wants you to rehearse a new song for the performance tonight," the assistant manager told her as the duellists left the stage.

"Another song?" repeated Dorinda in some dismay. "And for tonight? Oh, very well. I hope that it's something I already know. What's the name of it?"

"Desmond says it's just the thing for the first act: a very pretty Scottish ballad, 'The Bonny Earl of Murray.'"

"I do know the song," said Dorinda blankly. "But what possible connection does it have with *The Lady of the Lake*? Well, of course, my second act song, 'Lord Douglas' doesn't have anything to do with *The Lady of the Lake* either, but at least Lord Douglas has the same family name as the heroine!"

"Come, now, Miss Conroy, the Earl of Murray was Scottish, wasn't he?" replied Jack Wright easily. "That's enough connection for the audience. *They* don't care what you sing, just so the songs have a pretty melody and a pleasant rhyme."

After Dorinda had sung through several plaintive verses of 'The Bonny Earl of Murray'—"Ye *Highlands* and ye *Lawlands*, Oh! where ha'e ye been: They ha'e slain the Earl of *Murray*, And they laid him on the Green"—she left the stage for her small cramped dressing room, shaking her head at the treatment that Walter Scott's *The Lady of the Lake* was receiving at Desmond's cavalier hands. Because the new play could have only three acts to conform with the definition of a burletta and because of the inclusion of so many songs and dances, much of Scott's poetry had had to be cut from the playing version. In addition, to compensate for being unable to play the swashbuckling Roderick Dhu, Desmond had considerably padded his role of the aging minstrel, Allan-bane. He had also felt it necessary to add much dialogue to the part of Blanche of Devon, played most resentfully and unwillingly by Cassandra Bell, Desmond's leading actress, who was not even attempting to hide her jealousy at being supplanted by Dorinda.

In the dressing room, Dorinda slipped into a long, loose white dress, made with wide, flowing sleeves and conforming to the style of no particular period. Then she fastened a broad tartan sash diagonally across her bodice. She had protested to Desmond that she was sure her costume was nothing like the dress worn by a sixteenth-century Scottish clanswoman, but he had brushed aside her comments.

"Lord, Dorinda, there's no need to be so pickish about your costume," he had said nonchalantly. "Why, up until a few years ago, we actors wore on stage whatever was fashionable at the time. Garrick used to play Macbeth in a bag wig and knee breeches! It's a little different nowadays, of course. We wear garments that suggest the period or the place, or at least something that's not too conventional or contemporary. You'll be the perfect Ellen Douglas in that dress."

Smiling in amusement at the remembrance of Desmond's remarks on costuming, Dorinda began to paint her face, a task at which she had been gradually acquiring greater proficiency in the ten days since *The Lady of the Lake* had begun at the New Road Theatre in Brighton. Satisfied with her handiwork, she pinned back her dark hair and carefully adjusted over it the long golden locks of her wig. She stood up, surveying herself critically in the wavy, spotted mirror. There was no doubt about it, she thought with satisfaction. Even seen close up, there was nothing about Rachel Conroy, with her rouged cheeks and boldly painted lips and ridiculous but romantically flowing blond hair, to suggest the demure, well-mannered Dorinda Hayle.

She voiced an absent-minded "Come in" to a knock at her door, and was still looking at her image in the mirror when Desmond came into the room, already dressed in the sober gray mantle of Allan-bane. His limp had decidedly improved even in the short time that Dorinda had known him.

"You know, Desmond, you were right. I doubt that my own mother would recognize me in this costume," said Dorinda. "Well, naturally, Mama knows full well that I'm appearing as Ellen, but you understand what I mean."

"I'm *always* right—or nearly always, at least in stage matters," replied Desmond with an impudent grin. "Though why you're so set on hiding behind that dreadful wig—My good girl, you don't seem to realize just how talented you are. We've been doing such good business—there's another practically full house out there tonight—that I'm thinking of extending the run for at least another week. Maybe two. For that matter, I'm beginning to believe that *The Lady of the Lake* might do very well on 'Surreyside.' Wouldn't you like to shed Rachel Conroy to become the toast of London under your own name?"

"I wouldn't care to be the toast of London under *any* name. Don't forget, I agreed to play Ellen only for a limited time, at most until your company completes its spring circuit. And Cassandra Bell was hinting just yesterday that she expects to take over the part of Ellen as soon as her throat is better."

"Oh, Cassie. Her ideas are too big for her bonnet." Desmond dismissed Cassandra with a wave of his hand. "She's also madly jealous of you. Haven't you noticed?"

Dorinda turned toward him. "I can understand Cassandra's feelings. She's had years of experience on the stage, and she was your leading actress before I came along."

"I don't mean professional jealousy, and you know it, Dorinda. Cassie is jealous of you as a woman."

Dorinda looked at him steadily. "She has no reason to be. Not if you're referring to my relationship with you." She felt a twinge of uneasiness as Desmond moved closer to her in the tiny room and placed his hands on her shoulders. He had always behaved to her with the breezy unconventionality that she attributed to his free-and-easy theatrical background, but of late there had been a distinctly flirtatious note in his dealings with her.

"Sure and you can't be as hard-hearted as you sound," said Desmond cajolingly, with a hint of the brogue that betrayed his Irish ancestry. He tightened his grip on her shoulders, smiling down at her. "You won't deny, will you, that you like me just a little? Because I must tell you, my darlin' girl, that I've quite lost my heart to you. We could be a great partnership, the two of us. Mrs. Siddons and her brother, John Kemble, are both getting a bit long in the tooth. Why shouldn't you and I take their places one day?"

"I can think of several reason why not. For one thing, I don't have Mrs. Siddons' talent. For another, I have no

intention of making the stage a lifelong career. You know
very well that I agreed to take this role only because I'm
temporarily short of funds."

"By Jove, you may not have Sarah Siddons' talent—not
yet, perhaps—but you're twice as beautiful, and quite, quite
irresistible," said Desmond, his eyes kindling. Sliding his
arms around her, he bent his head to kiss her.

Pulling free, Dorinda boxed him smartly on the ear. "I'm
quite fond of you, Desmond, as a friend. Whether we remain
friends—and professional associates—is really up to you."

Massaging his ear, Desmond said ruefully, "Well, you're
in prime twig, aren't you? If you were a man I daresay you'd
be very handy with your fives!" He shrugged his shoulders
resignedly. "My darlin' girl, I apologize abjectly. I wouldn't
want to lose either your friendship or your theatrical services for a king's ransom. In future, I promise to be a perfect
gentleman."

"Apology accepted," said Dorinda with a forgiving smile,
and then, as she heard the callboy making his rounds, she
took one last glance in the mirror and moved into the wings
to await her first entrance.

The ten days' run in the role of Ellen Douglas had done
very little to lessen Dorinda's nervousness at the beginning
of each performance, and tonight was no exception. She was
well into her first scene with Fitz-James, and had finished
singing the dirgelike "Soldier, rest! thy warfare o'er, Sleep
the sleep that knows not breaking," before she could calm
her racing pulse and become aware of her audience as more
than a blurred and faceless mass.

The New Road Theatre was not large, but it was a
handsome structure with a roomy pit and gallery and two
tiers of boxes hung with gold-fringed draperies. As
Desmond had informed Dorinda, there was almost a full
house already, indicating that there would be few places
available at the "Second Price" in mid-evening. As Dorinda

moved to the front of the apron to sing "The Bonny Earl of Murray," she noted that somebody was even occupying the regent's box on the left, the one separated from the others by a gilt-iron latticework. This was the first time that she had seen the box occupied, and she flashed a frankly curious glance at the man sitting in it. He was a gentleman of about thirty-five, with fair hair and rather hawklike features, and as he noticed Dorinda's eyes upon him, he lifted his quizzing glass and surveyed her leisurely from head to toe with a careless insolence that made her cheeks burn beneath her paint.

As she finished her song and moved downstage, she murmured to Desmond, accompanying her on his harp as the minstrel Allan-bane, "Can that be the regent in his box?"

"Shouldn't think so. The regent must be pushing fifty, and I hear that he's gotten very fat," murmured Desmond in reply. "Must be a member of his household."

Out of the corner of her eye, Dorinda could observe that the man in the regent's box continued to stare at her with a discomforting intensity, and thereafter she tried to ignore him, avoiding any eye contact. But later in the act, as she joined the chorus in singing the famous boat song, "*Hail to the Chief*," she became aware that she was the object of still another unusually close scrutiny. She looked up into the box on the right next to the stage to find herself staring into a pair of lazily narrowed dark eyes set in a handsome, faintly bored face framed by a fashionably disheveled crop of black hair. The man brought his hands up in a gesture of soundless clapping while his lips formed the word *Brava*. Momentarily disconcerted, Dorinda lost the beat of the music and stumbled over the next line of the song. Her eyes flashed angrily at the man's knowing, amused little smile, and she turned her head abruptly and moved away from the box.

After the last act of *The Lady of the Lake*, Dorinda

escaped to her dressing room with a distinct feeling of relief.
She was dissatisfied with her performance tonight, and she
was glad that it was over. She was also nursing a grievance
against the two men in the boxes, who, by subjecting her to
their crossfire of boldly appraising stares, had distracted her
to the point of losing her concentration.

"Well, you'll be glad to know that I can now satisfy your
curiosity," announced Desmond, entering the dressing room
after a discreet knock.

"Oh? About what?"

"I thought that you wanted to know the identity of the
man in the regent's box. I was right when I guessed that he
was a member of the prince's household. He's Sir Fabian
Mordaunt, the regent's equerry. What's more, he wants to
talk to you."

Dorinda turned from the mirror to confront Desmond. "I
can imagine only one reason why—Sir Fabian, is that his
name?—would want to talk to me," she said coldy, "and the
answer is no."

"Now, wait a moment, Dorinda, it's not what you think. I
mean, for all I know, Mordaunt may be a loose fish—well,
dash it, it stands to reason he is, all that crowd around the
regent are out and outers, up to every rig and row in town.
But tonight he just wants to interview you on a professional
basis."

"What do you mean, professional?"

"I think that he wants to engage you to sing at one of the
regent's social evenings. No, don't shake your head and
refuse the offer before it's even made. You'd receive a very
nice fee for singing, and it might even be the beginning of a
larger career for you."

"I keep telling you that I have no intention of pursuing a
permanent career—"

"I know, I know," said Desmond hastily. "But will you at
least listen to the man? That can't hurt you, can it? Ten

minutes of your time? He might even ask *me* to perform, if you were to suggest it to him. And don't forget, favorable mention by the regent's equerry can't do my company any harm, either."

"Oh, very well, I'll see Sir Fabian. Mind, I don't promise anything."

"Fair enough. I'll clear the Green Room so that you and Mordaunt can have a little privacy."

Dorinda looked at Desmond, aghast. "But you mustn't do that," she protested. "The others in the company will resent being forced out of the Green Room, and rightly so."

Desmond gazed around the tiny dressing room. "You can hardly receive Mordaunt here. Not enough room to swing a cat."

Feeling suddenly that she wanted a bit more space between herself and Sir Fabian Mordaunt than the dressing room afforded, Dorinda capitulated. "Very well. I'll see him in the Green Room then. It will only be for ten minutes or so, after all, not long enough to cause too much inconvenience to the company. Tell Sir Fabian that I'll be with him in a few moments."

"Rather longer than that, won't it be? You're a quick change, I grant you that, but not that quick."

"Oh, I don't intend to change."

"Good God, Dorinda," Desmond exploded, "I've humored you in the matter of that ghastly wig, because from a distance—from the audience viewpoint—it doesn't look too ramshackle. But you're never going to make a cake of yourself by wearing it to an interview with the regent's equerry! What if you're offered, and accept, an engagement to sing at the Pavilion? Will you insist on wearing that abomination before the regent and his guests?"

"Well, perhaps not this wig. Surely I could find a more presentable short version for a personal appearance . . . provided, of course, that Sir Fabian extends the invitation, and I accept it."

Desmond sounded even more irritated as he said, "Now you're being really caper witted. I realize, though the Lord knows that I don't understand why, that you don't want anyone to know that you're appearing on the stage. But don't you see that you're carrying the matter much too far? There's no danger of Sir Fabian's recognizing you. He has never seen you before in his life. Nor has anyone else in the regent's circle. And just how likely is it that any of your acquaintances from Eastfield will be invited to be the regent's guest at the Pavilion?"

At Dorinda's stubborn silence, Desmond threw up his hands. "Do as you like then. I'll bring Mordaunt to the Green Room."

Still in her golden wig and long white gown, Dorinda was already beginning to feel slightly foolish as she walked into the Green Room several minutes later. Desmond was probably right, she thought. She was allowing her fear of being recognized as an actress to mount into an obsession. There was little chance that the vicar or Squire and Mrs. Cowleigh or Doctor Kenton would be among the audience at the New Road Theatre, and none at all that they would be invited to the Pavilion. An uncomfortable thought stirred in her mind: It was obvious that Desmond was beginning to equate her desire to remain incognito with a rejection of himself and his company. Perhaps she was being unrealistic, she told herself suddenly. Perhaps she should give up her tenuous membership in the world of the Quality, which she had attained upon her mother's marriage to Lord Roger, and grasp at the theatrical success that Desmond had assured her might be hers.

As a result of this brief bout of self-revelation, Dorinda was already more inclined to be gracious to Sir Fabian than she would have been a little earlier, and she was agreeably surprised to see, as he rose to greet her, that his attitude and his manners were unexceptional.

Seen close up, Sir Fabian Mordaunt's strong features seemed less harsh, even quite attractive, and he had a smile of considerable charm. His fair hair was arranged in the latest mode, and he wore a well-cut coat of *corbeau*-colored superfine and sage green kerseymere breeches.

Upon observing Dorinda's wig and costume, he looked somewhat startled, but he smiled, saying, "Pray allow me to compliment you on your singing and your stage presence, Miss Conroy. Your manager tells me that this is your first professional engagement. Yours would be a remarkable performance under any circumstance, in my humble opinion."

Dorinda bowed her head. "Thank you, Sir Fabian."

"I believe that Mr. Barry has informed you that I am the Prince Regent's equerry? His Royal Highness has a great interest in his future Scottish subjects, and it struck me as I listened to you sing that lovely Scottish ballad—what was it, 'The Bonny Earl of Murray'?—that he would much enjoy hearing you also. He has just arrived in Brighton, and I with him, for a few days to arrange for some alterations in the Marine Pavilion. Have you visited the Pavilion, Miss Conroy?"

"I've never been inside it. I've admired the exterior, of course."

"The Pavilion is one of the great passions of the prince's life. He's been building and rebuilding it for almost twenty-five years. There's a glass passage in the southern wing, painted with Chinese flowers, insects, fruits, and flowers and lighted from without, that is one of my favorite corners of the building. It always makes me imagine that I am walking through a huge Chinese lantern. Quite lovely. Would you be interested in being part of the entertainment after a small dinner party that His Highness is giving on Thursday? The fee, I might add, will be quite generous. Twenty-five guineas."

Dorinda's eyes widened at the abruptness of the request, even though she had been expecting it, and at the size of the suggested gratuity. "Thank you, I would be delighted to sing," she said, making a quick decision. "I wonder . . . Mr. Barry did tell you that I'm a neophyte actress, and I'm just a little nervous at the thought of performing for His Royal Highness. Would it be possible for Mr. Barry to accompany me to the Pavilion? Perhaps even to sing there himself?"

"No problem at all. I should be quite delighted to arrange it," replied Sir Fabian promptly.

"Well, then, Sir Fabian, if that's all?" said Dorinda, rising. "Mr. Barry and I will come to the Pavilion immediately after our performance here on Thursday, if that is satisfactory."

"More than satisfactory," said Sir Fabian, rising also. "And now that we have that business out of the way, my dear, we can proceed to more important matters."

Dorinda, who had turned away and was about to leave the room, paused in surprise. "I don't think that I understand. What important matters?"

Sir Fabian came up close to her. "Oh, come now, don't play the green girl with me. You must have guessed that I came here wearing two hats," he drawled with an unpleasantly familiar grin. "One in my capacity as royal equerry: The regent really does like to present new talent to his guests, nor would he be averse to enjoying your company in other ways, I think, even though his tastes have turned more to elderly charmers these days. But I don't pander for him. I let Colonel MacMahon take care of that. No, I'm wearing my second hat in my own interests. Yours, too, I hope."

He paused, raking her face and body with a long, hatefully approving glance, before continuing, "You see, my dear Rachel, I've taken quite a fancy to you. You not only have a lovely singing voice, a beautiful face and a fine figure, but you have a decided air of gentility. I'd like to discuss with you the possibility of coming to a permanent arrangement—well, for the next year or two, shall we say? How would you like your own little house in London, your own carriage, a generous dress allowance? A good deal of your time would be your own, I might add. My duties with His Royal Highness would keep me from your side—oh, very reluctantly!—for much of the time. Well? How does my proposition strike you? Are you at all interested?"

Sir Fabian arched an expectant eyebrow. It was clear from his manner that his question was no more than a formality; quite obviously he believed that Dorinda would snap at his bait. She had allowed him to speak without interruption largely because anger had turned her speechless, but now she exploded.

"No, I am *not* interested, sir. On the contrary, I am insulted to the core by your 'proposition.' What made you think that I was on the catch for a protector? No matter. Whatever your reason, I don't care to hear it. Good-bye, sir."

Sir Fabian caught her arm as she turned to leave. "Now, now, my dear, don't be so top-lofty. I see now that I may have been a little blunt in my approach to you. A high flyer like yourself wants a bit more finesse from her admirers, wants to be coaxed a little," he said with a knowing chuckle.

Dorinda shook off his hand. "You're very much mistaken, Sir Fabian. Even if I were the light skirt you take me for, even if you had courted me with the gallantry of Casanova himself, I would reject your offer. To put it quite bluntly, I don't like you. I would rather beg on the streets than live under the protection of a man with so little breeding."

"A vixen like you wouldn't know a man of breeding if she met one," snarled Sir Fabian, his face flushed an angry red.

"I think that I'll just have to give you a lesson in how to speak to your betters."

He advanced on her purposefully, and Dorinda, moving away without thought to the position of the two doors, found herself cornered near the fireplace. Sir Fabian paused several feet away from her, his lips curved in an ugly grin. "I take back my offer, my girl, but before I leave I'm going to show you what you'll be missing."

In one fluid motion, Dorinda picked up a poker from beside the fireplace and interposed it between herself and Sir Fabian.

"Do you really think that you can stop me with that thing?" Sir Fabian gibed, and made a quick lunge to seize the poker. Nimbly twisting away, Dorinda raised the poker and brought it down on his shoulder with all her force as he rushed by her and slammed into the mantel. Slowly he turned from the fireplace, looking down incredulously at his elegant coat, the fine *corbeau*-colored cloth of which was ripped and blackened at the right shoulder. "Look what you've done," he said blankly. "This is a new coat, I just got it from the tailor last week—and I think that you may have broken my collarbone."

"I'm sorry if I've hurt you, but it's really your own fault. I'd like you to leave now, please."

"Don't you order me around, miss," snapped Sir Fabian, wincing as he inadvertently moved his injured shoulder. "I'll leave when I damned well please. You don't think that I'm going to stand still for what you've done, do you?"

"If you don't leave this room immediately, I'll hit you again," Dorinda exclaimed, raising the poker threateningly.

"You wouldn't dare—" Sir Fabian broke off, eying Dorinda uneasily as she moved toward him with an ever-quickening step. At the last moment, just as she drew a deep breath and brought the poker up, he turned tail, fumbling momentarily at the doorknob with an unpracticed left hand before he wrenched the door open and plunged into the corridor. There, he careened into a tall figure standing just outside the door and fell headlong to the floor.

The tall newcomer brought his quizzing glass to his eye and looked from Dorinda, still with the poker in hand, to the sprawled figure of Sir Fabian, who laboriously got to his feet by dint of bracing himself against the wall with his uninjured left arm.

"By George, Mordaunt, I'd heard that you were in the petticoat line, and I know that you fancy yourself as a pretty fighter for an amateur," the man drawled, "but I never realized that you advocated performing both activities at the same time. Perhaps with a little more practice? . . . "

Sir Fabian's high color faded to a sickly pallor. "If this doxy hadn't half crippled me, I'd make you pay instanter for what you just said," he grated to the newcomer. "But don't think that I'll forget it. As for you"—he turned to Dorinda with a glare of such malevolence that she took a step backward—"as for you, my girl, you'll be sorry to your dying day that you crossed me."

"That's enough, Mordaunt. Better leave while you're still in one piece," said the stranger in a tone of cold authority.

Throwing one last glance of pure hatred at Dorinda, Sir Fabian stumbled off down the corridor.

"Now, Miss—Conroy, is that correct?—are you all right? That fellow Mordaunt didn't hurt you?"

Feeling suddenly very tired, Dorinda stared down at the poker in vague surprise. She would have found it hard to believe that she had actually hit Sir Fabian with enough force to break his collarbone if it had not been for the wisp of *corbeau*-colored thread clinging to the head of the poker. Compressing her lips, she went into the Green Room and marched to the fireplace to return the poker to its proper place. Turning, she faced the stranger who had followed her into the room, and said, "I'm quite all right, sir. Thank you for your assistance in ridding me of Sir Fabian, although—"

"Although you had already successfully fended him off, with no need whatsoever of any help from me," finished the stranger with a smile.

Dorinda looked closely at the handsome, faintly bored face, at the lazily narrowed dark eyes, at the tall, rangy, graceful figure in the magnificently tailored black evening coat, white breeches, and masterfully tied cravat, and realized that here was no stranger. This was the man who had sat in the box opposite Sir Fabian in the theatre tonight, and who, quite as much as Sir Fabian, had contributed to the discomfiture that had caused her to give a less than satisfactory performance.

"Did you really hit Mordaunt with that poker?" the man asked, a coolly appreciative smile playing around his well-shaped mouth.

"I did," replied Dorinda coldly.

"I'm sure that he deserved it. He always was a dull dog, a glass-cocker of a fellow."

Dorinda lifted an eyebrow. "That's as may be, but it's scarcely something I care to discuss with you, sir. Will you excuse me?" Bowing slightly, she turned and was halfway to the door leading to the dressing rooms when the man spoke again.

"Before you go, won't you let me tell you how much I enjoyed your singing?"

Hesitating, Dorinda turned back and walked several steps toward the center of the room. "Thank you. I'm glad that you enjoyed the play."

"Oh, the play. It's no better and no worse than the other versions of *The Lady of the Lake*. Poor Scott. The dramatists seize on his work the moment that it's off the press, and he has no control at all over what they do with it. No, your singing, Miss Conroy, was the bright spot of this production.

All the more delightful for me, because I was stranded here in Brighton this evening—my curricle was damaged in an encounter with the cow-handed driver of a gig—and I had resigned myself to a solitary dinner and to dipping rather too deeply into a brandy bottle when I thought to attend the performance tonight. Have you ever considered singing in opera? I can hear that your voice isn't professionally trained, but the quality is there."

"Thank you again, but no, I have no desire to sing in opera."

"A pity. With proper training, you might go far. And a classical music career would certainly be remunerative. I understand that Catalani was paid two thousand pounds for her first full season at the King's Theatre some years ago, and received even larger sums from benefit performances and other concerts."

"I'm sure that opera singers are very well paid, but an operatic career is not for me."

"But why ever not? If it's because you don't know where to go for training, or if you lack the funds . . . look here, Miss Conroy, I should be delighted to help you. Just say the word."

Dorinda froze. Here was another proof, if she needed it, that polite society equated the professional actress or singer with the demimonde. This handsome, self-assured Corinthian, though neither in manner nor in speech did he convey that odious sense of familiarity so evident in Sir Fabian Mordaunt, would never behave so unconventionally, much less offer financial assistance, to any female of his own class.

"I thank you, sir, but I have no need of your money," replied Dorinda. She could hear the beginning strains of the music for the latter part of the *Chinese Harlequinade*, and the sounds of movement from the dressing room area increased. "Pray excuse me. The second half of the bill is about to start, and I have deprived my fellow players of the Green Room for long enough."

"Please wait, just a moment." The stranger put his *chapeau bras* and his stick on a table and walked over to her. "You must do as you like about accepting my offer to fund your musical training, of course—incidentally, the offer will remain open indefinitely—but in the meantime, won't you give me the opportunity to be your friend?"

Eying him warily, Dorinda backed away slightly. "What do you mean by 'friend'?"

He spread his hands in a deprecating gesture. "Ah, Miss Conroy, must we be so crass, so unromantic? I daresay that Mordaunt spelled out all the words and crossed all his ts, but as for me . . . shall we just say that I would like to know you a little better? Then later, definitely later, after I've discovered the beauties that I know must be under that dreadful wig and all that paint . . ." He put a light hand on the wig, and then, as Dorinda tried to jerk away, he caught her in his arms and kissed her lingeringly on the mouth.

Dorinda had had very little experience of kissing. There had been several inexpert stolen busses by young Martin Cowleigh, the squire's son, and earlier this evening Desmond's fumbled attempt. But Dorinda had never felt as she did now, clasped in this man's arms, smelling the faint scent of freshly laundered linen and expensive brandy, her lips throbbing with a deliciously enticing warmth while every bone in her body seemed to dissolve away so that, for support, she clung to his tautly muscled frame.

"There," he murmured, after long moments had slipped away. "That's what I meant." He lifted his head, smiling down at her, his eyes no longer lazy but kindling with an ever-growing spark.

Dorinda looked up at him blankly, experiencing momentarily the odd sensation that she had just awakened in strange surroundings after a sound sleep. Then, her face twisting in self-dislike, she raked her hand across his face and pulled away from him.

Reaching inside his sleeve for a handkerchief, he mopped at his cheek, examining the red-splotched linen with a calmly detached air.

"My dear Miss Conroy, there was really no need for such vehemence," he observed. "A mere word from you would have effected my dismissal, I assure you. I am not in the habit of inflicting myself on reluctant females. Unlike poor Mordaunt, I have never pressed my suit so eagerly that the object of my attentions felt it necessary to resort to a poker. Now, it really does look as though we have very little more to say to each other, so good evening to you and may I extend my best wishes for your future career."

Bowing, he picked up his hat and stick, and still holding the handkerchief to his bleeding face, left the room.

Clenching her fists, Dorinda barely restrained herself from bursting into tears. She was not sorry, exactly, for scratching the stranger's face. He had, after all, deserved something for treating her like a common slattern. But she did regret the lack of fastidiousness that had allowed her to remain locked compliantly in his embrace, and she regretted her own lack of self-control in striking out at him with her fingernails.

"By all that's holy, Dorinda, what have you been up to?" demanded Desmond as he hurried into the Green Room moments after the stranger had departed. "First the regent's equerry comes howling to me, complaining that you assaulted him with a poker—my God, Dorinda, do you realize that you've probably broken the poor man's shoulder or arm?—and then when I come to the Green Room to find out exactly what happened, I observe through the open door that you're having an interview with still another swell. And a few minutes after *that*, this second admirer of yours bursts through the door mopping a face that you seem to have scratched to ribbons! What about your engagement to sing at the Pavilion?"

"We'll just have to forget about singing for the regent," replied Dorinda wearily. "Sir Fabian made it quite clear that the engagement was contingent upon my accepting another purely personal proposition. That's when I hit him with the poker. As for the second gentleman, while his manner may have been somewhat more genteel, he had much the same kind of future in mind for me that Sir Fabian did. I wish that I had thought to use the poker on him too!"

Desmond whistled. "Well, I *am* sorry, my dear. I certainly didn't suspect that Sir Fabian was such a loose fish. And of course I hadn't a notion that the other swell even wanted to see you." He sighed. "An engagement at the Marine Pavilion would have been a real feather in your cap, but . . . well, no matter. There will be other opportunities for someone with your talent."

"No, there won't," exclaimed Dorinda, coming to a quick decision. "Desmond, I must tell you this: I intend to leave the company at the end of the week—permanently. I find that I don't fancy a stage career even temporarily. Cassandra Bell will be well enough in a few days to take over my role."

"But, Dorinda, you can't mean that," protested Desmond. "I realize that you've just had a somewhat unpleasant experience—"

"A somewhat unpleasant experience! And in the singular!" Dorinda exploded. "My dear, Desmond, I've been attacked on three separate occasions in one evening by males who appear to think that, by appearing on stage, I have automatically entered the ranks of the Fashionable Impures. That kind of harassment is too great a price to pay for a theatrical career, and I want no more of it."

"Well, by George, if that ain't coming it much too

strong," exclaimed an aggrieved Desmond. "I don't blame you for sending those two bang-up bloods to the rightabout, but dash it, Dorinda, I just tried to kiss you!"

"Oh, I'm sorry, Desmond, I shouldn't have classed you with those two—those two loose screws," said Dorinda remorsefully. "But that's really beside the point. I just don't want to appear on the stage any longer, and I don't think that there is anything you could say that would make me change my mind."

Chapter III

Dorinda paused, the feather duster poised in her hand as she watched little Elspeth Hubbard, her former maid of all work, trudge down the lane past the drawing-room window. Most regretfully, she had let Elspeth go the previous week after she had returned from Brighton at the end of her brief stage career, and today, in an unbecoming mobcap and enveloping apron, she was performing Elspeth's duties.

Dorinda had dismissed Elspeth in an effort to pare down the household expenses even further. It was true that Desmond had paid her a generous five pounds for her scant two weeks at the theatre, and there still remained a small sum saved from her accounts over the past year, but the money would not last indefinitely. She must obtain employment as soon as possible. Only yesterday she had received a letter from the headmistress of her former school, promising to be on the lookout for a position as governess. But Miss Adams had also said quite frankly that, if asked, she would feel obliged to reveal the details of Dorinda's background and parentage.

Pausing again, Dorinda stared absently at the small framed watercolor, a favorite of Lord Roger's, which hung over the fireplace. Had she done the right thing, turning her back on Desmond's acting company and a modest but assured income for the remainder of the winter touring season? True, it would have been difficult for Charlotte to maintain for long the fiction that Dorinda was visiting friends; the vicar's wife and Mrs. Cowleigh, the wife of the squire, knew all too well how limited was the Wingate social circle. And no doubt she would have been frequently obliged to fend off amorous advances from the bored young blades in the audiences, though probably none of these would-be suitors would have been quite as obnoxious as Sir Fabian Mordaunt.

A knock sounded at the front entrance of the cottage, but Dorinda continued her dusting until she remembered belatedly that Elspeth was no longer in her employ. Dorinda rushed to open the door, her eyes widening as she gazed at the tall, imposing, rather stout lady, clad in a dark blue velvet pelisse and a hat bedecked with huge ostrich plumes, who stood on the doorstep. Behind her, at the garden gate, was a handsome chaise drawn by four horses. A modishly dressed young lady peered out of the window of the chaise.

"Good afternoon," said the lady. "I wish to see Miss Hayle, Miss Dorinda Hayle, please."

"Oh." Dorinda cast a flustered look down at her apron. "I am Miss Hayle. May I help you?"

The lady arched an eyebrow in surprise. "How do you do, Miss Hayle," she began, her tone revealing faint displeasure. "May I come in to talk to you? I am the Dowager Marchioness of Torrington."

"Lady Torrington!" Dorinda gasped. "Oh, yes. Please come in." She stood aside to allow Lady Torrington to enter, whisking off her cap and apron and smoothing her hair as she added, "I apologize for my appearance, but we keep no servants now, and I was doing the dusting." Dorinda glanced back at the carriage. "Would the young lady care to come in too? It's rather brisk out today."

"No. My granddaughter will remain in the carriage. I wish to speak to you alone," said the dowager, following Dorinda into the drawing room.

"As you wish. Please have a chair. I expect that you've come to pay a condolence call. If you'll wait just a moment, I'll tell my mother that you're here."

"I do not wish to see your mother, Miss Hayle. I never recognized her as a member of my family during my son's lifetime, and I do not propose to do so now. As I indicated to you at the door, I have come here to talk to you."

Stifling the quick, angry retort that rose to her lips at Lady Torrington's contemptuous reference to Charlotte, Dorinda sat down opposite the dowager. As the minutes dragged by, Dorinda became increasingly nervous under Lady Torrington's intent, silent stare.

"I will be quite frank with you," said the dowager at last. "I've come here to see you because of a letter I received recently from your lawyer, Mr. Stowe, a letter in which he asked me to consider the possibility of granting a yearly allowance to your mother. Mr. Stowe stated that my son and his wife had been living a quiet, respectable life here for many years. He also said, Miss Hayle, that much of the credit for this family respectability and good repute here in the village is due to your excellent qualities as a manager and to your well-marked common sense."

"Mr. Stowe is very kind," replied Dorinda, mildly embarrassed. "I hope that he also told you that I myself do not want or expect anything from you. I can take care of myself, but it would be most considerate and generous of you to provide for Mama."

Lady Torrington eyed her curiously. "You say that you don't want anything from me. Supposing I did grant your mother an allowance just sufficient for her own needs? What would you do then, left to your own resources?"

"I believe myself to be reasonably well educated," replied Dorinda composedly, curbing a stab of resentment at Lady Torrington's brusque approach. In this conversation, she thought, her pride would have to take second place. She must avoid antagonizing the dowager. "I've been thinking of obtaining a position as governess or as a companion. Or I daresay that I could always—" She stopped abruptly, choking back the rest of the sentence. She had been about to say, "I could always go back to the stage," but she sensed instinctively that Lady Torrington's faint interest in helping Charlotte would evaporate if the dowager learned about Dorinda's appearances at the New Road Theatre. "I might try for a position as assistant in one of the Brighton shops," she ended lamely.

"Not the most enviable way of earning one's livelihood, I fear. You are well spoken, Miss Hayle. Where did you attend school?"

"I attended Miss Adams' Academy in Tunbridge Wells. It wasn't the best or the most fashionable school in England, but one could learn if one put one's mind to it. And I spent a good deal of my time with my stepfather, talking and reading. Perhaps you've forgotten that your son was a cultivated man."

There was a quiver at the corner of Lady Torrington's mouth. After a moment she said, "Yes, he was a cultivated man—when he wasn't drowning himself in gin." She lapsed into a brooding silence, rousing herself at length to say, "Mr. Stowe's letter did cause me to wonder if I were being overly harsh to your mother. I came here to see for myself where and how my son's widow was living—but I came mostly to see you. You see, I thought if, after I spoke to you,

you lived up to Mr. Stowe's very flattering description, I might myself offer you a position."

Dorinda could only stare at the dowager in surprise.

"Yes, I've quite made up my mind," said the marchioness, squaring her shoulders. "I would like you to act as companion to my granddaughter, Lady Letitia Wingate, who will be coming out this spring. Her parents are both dead, drowned in a Channel crossing some years ago after they had paid a visit to Paris during the Peace of Amiens, and Letty's brother Richard, the present Lord Torrington, is very young, still a schoolboy at Eton. So Letty is in my complete charge, and I simply feel disinclined to chaperone her through an entire London season. I'm too old, for one thing, and I suffer from a bad case of the gout. Well, Miss Hayle? Do you feel disposed to take this on? If you do and if you succeed in guiding Letty through the pitfalls of her first season, I will see to it that your mother receives an allowance for the rest of her life, and I am prepared to settle on you a sum that will give you at least a modest independence." She named an amount that made Dorinda catch her breath.

"I don't know what to say, Lady Torrington," said Dorinda after a dazed pause. "I've never moved in fashionable society. Quite truthfully, I doubt that I would be of the slightest use to Lady Letitia as a chaperon. It would almost be a case of the blind leading the blind."

"Don't worry about your lack of social experience. I'll be with you and Letty in London, advising you, giving you pointers. In fact, the ultimate responsibility for my granddaughter will be mine. It's just that I don't wish to be in constant attendance on Letty, paying calls, going to nightly balls, shopping." The marchioness hesitated. "I must tell you, Letty is somewhat hard to handle. In fact, she's a real hoyden in many ways. She will talk to anybody, anywhere, and she strikes up the most inappropriate acquaintances—

or worse. Not long ago her then governess caught her kissing one of the stable grooms." Lady Torrington reddened in embarrassment. "And above all," she continued, "Letty is horse mad. She insists on riding to hounds, for example, which certainly wasn't done in my day. Not many ladies choose to do so even today. I am making a special point of telling you all this, because it is essential that Letty not spoil her season with some kind of foolish, unnecessary indiscretion that could ruin her future, something that could prevent her from making the marriage of the year, the decade. For, if all goes as planned, she will marry the Duke of Shalford in the autumn."

"I see. I daresay that would be a very great thing for Lady Letitia, being a duchess," ventured Dorinda.

"Not just any duchess," retorted the dowager impatiently. "Have you never heard of the Dukedom of Shalford? It is among the oldest dukedoms in England, being second only to that of Norfolk. And the present duke is very probably the richest man in the country. Certainly he is one of the great leaders of fashion."

"Indeed. Like Beau Brummell."

"Certainly not," exclaimed Lady Torrington witheringly. "Who, after all, is Brummell? His father was a government clerk and his grandfather a valet. What's more, the man can't remain a power in society much longer. He's fallen out with the regent, and according to the *on-dit*, he's under the hatches, in the hands of the cents-per-cent. No, Miss Hayle, as a leader of society, Brummell is only a pale shadow to Shalford."

"Oh," said Dorinda, taken aback. "Well, I can certainly understand now how . . . how distinguished a marriage this would be for Lady Letitia."

"And a very good match for Shalford, too," returned Lady Torrington instantly. "The Wingate patent of nobility, after all, goes back to the fourteenth century. But yes, I shall be very happy to see Letty safely married to Shalford, though I must say that it came about very unexpectedly." The Dowager nodded her head reminiscently. "We all thought, you see, that he was a hardened case, not at all on the catch for a wife, more than content to groom his young nephew as his heir. But then, last spring, when he was visiting friends near our estate in Leicestershire, he caught sight of Letty riding to hounds. Apparently he was instantly taken with her, and she with him, fortunately. But Shalford and I agreed that she was too young to marry just yet; she must have a London season to find herself, to grow a little more adult. So there will be no formal betrothal until the end of the season. In fact, Shalford prefers that even the unofficial engagement should be kept secret. He wants Letty to be perfectly free to change her mind about the marriage."

Dorinda hesitated. "Well, Lady Torrington, if you really think that I could carry out such duties . . ."

"I shouldn't otherwise have offered you the position. You have presence, you have common sense, and you are the right age—young enough to match Letty's rather exhausting supply of energy, old enough to have a wiser head. And now, I think perhaps it is time that you and Letty met. If you will just have your servant ask her to come in . . ."

"As I told you, we don't have a servant at present. I'll be happy to go out to the carriage myself. . . ." Glancing out the window, Dorinda paused, horrified, as she saw Desmond Barry in the act of helping a young woman, obviously Lady Letitia, out of the Wingate carriage and into his curricle. In a moment, the pair drove away, with Lady Letitia holding the reins.

"Lady Torrington, I hope this won't upset you too much . . . your granddaughter has just gone off for a drive with a . . . a friend of mine."

"Indeed. And who, pray, is this friend? What is his

family?" demanded the dowager in tones of deep displeasure.

"His name is Desmond Barry. He's . . ." It was on the tip of Dorinda's tongue to reveal that Desmond was an actor, but she checked herself. "Mr. Barry is an old friend of the family. Probably he has just heard of Lord Roger's death and has come to offer his condolences."

Lady Torrington sniffed. "What sort of gentleman can this friend of yours be, to cast out lures to a respectable young female? But there, it was probably all Letty's doing," she conceded honestly. "It's just like her, to go driving off with a complete stranger. Let it be a lesson to you, Miss Hayle. You will have to be on your guard at all times with Letty. Well, I suggest that we spend our time until she returns in settling the details of our arrangement. First of all, I do not wish it to be known that you are my son's stepdaughter. I think that we will introduce you as a distant connection of mine on my mother's side. One of my mother's cousins married a clergyman and went off to live in an obscure village in Northumberland near the Scottish border. I shall say you are one of Cousin Margaret's granddaughters, impoverished and in need of a position but perfectly respectable."

Lady Torrington raised an inquiring eyebrow, and Dorinda fought down a familiar surge of anger at the dowager's coolly arrogant slur on her parentage.

"It seems a harmless enough masquerade. I have no objection to being known as your cousin's granddaughter," Dorinda said quietly.

"Excellent. Now then, I suggest that you come to London at the end of March or the early part of April, well before the start of the season, so you can accustom yourself to living in the city, and also"—here the dowager gazed appraisingly at Dorinda's simple gown of black merino—"that you buy a new wardrobe. I realize you will be in first mourning for some time yet, but under the circumstances I would prefer that you do not wear black."

Wondering bleakly if the marchioness had ever even contemplated wearing mourning for Lord Roger's death, Dorinda merely replied, "As you wish." She caught the sound of hooves outside on the roadway and moved to the window, peering out as she said, "I believe that Lady Letitia and Mr. Barry have returned."

"Come along then, Miss Hayle. Let me introduce you to my granddaughter."

As Lady Torrington and Dorinda emerged from the cottage, Desmond Barry was just helping Lady Letitia out of the curricle in front of the gate.

"Oh, Grandmama, guess what?" the girl called as she caught sight of Lady Torrington. "I've just been driving Mr. Barry's curricle, and it's no more difficult, really, than driving my pony cart at home."

Lady Letitia Wingate was not really a beautiful girl, Dorinda decided; the young woman only gave the appearance of being so. She had tawny blond curls, large brown eyes, a short snub nose lightly dusted with freckles, a pretty but overly generous mouth, and a small slim graceful figure. No, she was not really beautiful, but the dancing lights in her brown eyes, the incandescence of her delightful smile, gave her an expression of warmth and vivacity that was superior to beauty.

"Oh, I'm quite prepared to believe that you drove this gentleman's curricle very expertly, my dear," said Lady Torrington dryly. "I've never doubted your skill with horses. Miss Hayle, this is my granddaughter, Lady Letitia Wingate. Letty, Miss Hayle will be your companion when we go to London for the season." The dowager flicked a frigid glance at Desmond. "You, sir, are Mr. Barry, I believe. I am the Marchioness of Torrington."

Bowing deeply, a rather overawed Desmond replied, "I

can certainly vouch for Lady Letitia's skill with the ribbons, your ladyship. She can drive to the inch."

"Oh, come now, Mr. Barry, that's doing it rather too brown," said Lady Letitia merrily. "I drove well enough, I suppose, but the ride would have been much better if your horses had been well matched. They should be exactly alike in size, color, and gait. Otherwise any equality in their pace will joggle the passengers."

Desmond threw up his hands with a grin. "You mustn't blame me too much, you know. These are just job horses that I hired from the livery stable."

Letty turned back to Lady Torrington. "Mr. Barry and I were having the most interesting conversation, Grandmama. He's an actor, and he's been telling me about his new musical version of *The Lady of the Lake*. Perhaps we could stay over an extra night in Brighton to see a performance."

Glancing in distress at Desmond, Dorinda was relieved to gather from his little nod of reassurance that he had not told Letty about Dorinda's involvement with his company. But her heart sank as Lady Torrington, frowning deeply, exclaimed, "Mr. Barry is an actor? Miss Hayle, I thought you said that he was an old friend of your family."

"Yes, I knew Lady Roger many years ago when she was a member of my father's company," said Desmond quickly. "I'm appearing now in Brighton with a new play, and when I chanced to hear about Lord Roger's death I naturally wanted to express my condo—"

"Yes, very well," said Lady Torrington, ruthlessly cutting Desmond short. "Miss Hayle, we must be going. Mr. Stowe, in Brighton, will be in contact with you concerning funds and the arrangements for your journey to London. Good day."

"Good-bye, Miss Hayle. I shall look forward to seeing you in London. And thank you, Mr. Barry, for letting me drive your curricle," Letty called back, favoring them with a dazzling smile as her grandmother shepherded her to the carriage.

"My eye and Betty Martin, so that's Lady Roger's mama-in-law," observed Desmond as he and Dorinda stood at the gate, watching the dowager's carriage disappear down the village street. "What a Tartar she looks to be. Did you notice how she treated me after she found out that I was an actor? She stared straight through me as if I weren't there at all! My dear girl, what do you think she would have said if I had told her that you and I had appeared on the stage together?"

Dorinda shivered. "Thank you for not telling her, or Lady Letitia either."

"Do give me a little credit for ordinary common sense, Dorinda. If you didn't want your neighbors here in Eastfield to know about your stage career, then you certainly didn't want Lord Roger's high and mighty family to find out about it. Now, what's this about your going to London?"

"Desmond, it's the most marvelous thing. I still can't quite believe it. Lady Torrington is going to continue Mama's allowance, and I'm to be Lady Letitia's companion during the coming London season. And if I perform my duties capably, Lady Torrington will settle a small permanent income on me. Just think of it, all my problems have been solved with just one whisk of her ladyship's magic wand!"

Shaking his head, Desmond said shrewdly, "This is the real world, Dorinda, not a fairy tale. There must be some reason for Lady Torrington's turnabout. What's the fly in the ointment?" He smiled suddenly, "It's Lady Letitia, isn't it? I'll warrant the girl will be a rare handful."

"What an unkind thing to say. She seems a very sweet, charming girl to me."

"Don't try to bam me. I may not mingle with the Ton, but even I know that young ladies of the Quality don't accept rides from complete strangers. No, Lady Torrington can't or won't cope with the chit herself, so she's handing the girl over to you."

Privately, Dorinda felt that there might be more than a grain of truth in Desmond's remark, but she said merely, "I'm not at all worried about Lady Letitia, Desmond. Now, what brings you to Eastfield today?"

"What if I said that I had come to try to persuade you to return to the company? Cassie simply doesn't have your voice or your stage presence—or your audience appeal. We haven't seen many full houses since you left us. I truly believe that you could have a real future in the theatre."

Dorinda shook her head. "No, I'm sorry. I want to put all that behind me."

"I rather thought that you would say that. My dearest, darling Dorinda, I simply hate to think of your being buried for the rest of your life in this dreary place—but there, I'm forgetting. You aren't going to stay here, are you? You're going to London, where you'll be hobnobbing with all the swells. Perhaps you really will be living in a fairy tale, my girl. You may meet your Prince Charming, or at the very least a duke or a marquess, and live happily ever after!"

"Now who's forgetting the real world?" demanded Dorinda with a laugh. "I'll be coming back here to Eastfield in the autumn—still very much a spinster, without a shadow of a doubt!—and be very happy to do so, I assure you. And if you bring your company to Brighton next season, you must be sure to call upon me and Mama."

"I'll certainly do that. I don't intend to lose sight of you, Dorinda. For now, though, I've come to say good-bye. We're moving on to Newhaven tomorrow."

"How is your leg? I notice that you're scarcely limping at all now."

"It's almost healed. I'll be returning to Covent Garden and Kemble's management before very long, I hope."

Desmond looked a little wistful as he added, "Will you come to see me perform in London, if I get a good role, that is? More than just a walk-on, or a spear-carrying part?"

Her expression softening, Dorinda put her hand lightly on his arm. "Dear Desmond, of course I will if I can. I hope to see you playing Hamlet and Macbeth and Othello!"

"Not much chance of that, but thank you." Desmond clasped both her hands in his. "I'll miss you, my dear." She pulled away as he made an instinctive move to kiss her, and he grinned ruefully. "I know. Mustn't scandalize the neighbors. Well, good-bye, Dorinda. Oh, I almost forgot to tell you. Perhaps you were wise not to continue acting with the company after you hit Sir Fabian Mordaunt with the poker. He came around next day, breathing fire, wanting to know how he could lay hands on you. Naturally, I told him that Miss Rachel Conroy had left town, gone Heaven knows where. And of course the rest of my company never knew your real name or where you live, so I think you're safe from the wicked baronet."

Chapter IV

As she gazed at her reflection in the full-length cheval glass, momentarily Dorinda had the startling impression that she was looking at a stranger. She had never worn anything as becoming—or as fashionable, or as expensive—as this dress which consisted of a yellow crepe underdress topped by a tunic of gold-colored spider net with an uneven hem line. She had a new coiffure too, an arrangement in the antique Roman style that she had seen in the *Lady's Monthly Museum Magazine*. At the back of her head, her hair was drawn together and confined in ringlets, while at the front, it was in full curl threaded by a gold bandeau.

She had changed more than her appearance; she had changed her entire way of life, she thought as she reflected rather unbelievingly on the events of the scant month since her arrival in London at the end of March. It seemed much longer than that since she had boarded the fast day coach in Brighton, to travel at the incredible speed of twelve miles an hour and to be deposited some five hours later in London at the famous coaching inn, the Golden Cross, across from Northumberland House.

Dorinda could smile now as she recalled her wide-eyed gawking at the colorful and bustling London street scene. A bewildering volume of vehicles competed with one another for room in the wide streets—brewers' drays, hooded wag-gons, hay carts, stagecoaches, curricles and tilburies, and phaetons—and the shop windows were crammed with an enticing variety of silks and china and jewels and silver. As she rode in a hackney cab to Berkeley Square, however, Dorinda had found herself even more fascinated by the human element, the Londoners themselves: ballad singers and peddlers, bakers in white aprons shouting "hot loaves," milkmaids crying their wares, street sweepers offering their services at every crossing, hawkers with bandboxes on poles, and many tattered, dirty, dispirited lost souls—men, women, and children—whose backgrounds or vocations she could only attempt to guess. Finally, there had been her rather nervous arrival at Torrington House. It was situated in Berkeley Square, a large oblong space planted with plane trees just coming into leaf, their foliage half hiding the square's garden and the charming summer house in its center. The stately, beautifully proportioned houses lining the square were separated from the street by arrow-headed iron railings which culminated in a graceful arch at each entrance, where an iron lantern hung over the steps.

In the weeks since her arrival in London, Dorinda had been too busy to be introspective. She had spent much of her time shopping, and being fitted for her extensive new ward-robe, all paid for by the dowager. She had also availed herself of the opportunity to view many of the London sights about which she had heard, and she and Lady Letitia had dutifully paid calls on those friends of Lady Torrington who had already arrived in town. But Dorinda had often thought back to Desmond Barry's remark that she had been chosen to act as Letty's companion because Lady Torrington found the girl hard to manage, and she had ruefully come to the conclusion that Desmond was right: Letty *was* a handful.

Dorinda sighed. Letty was a winsome, sunny-hearted girl who had in short order apparently come to feel a real affection for her new companion, but she required the closest of supervision. Letty loved people, all sorts of people, and it seemed to matter little to her whether her companions shared her own social standing or belonged to the lower classes. Once, Dorinda had found her down in the kitchens enthusiastically helping the cook make apricot tarts. Several times Dorinda had caught Letty hard at work in the stables, grooming her horses alongside the stable hands. Letty was inclined to talk volubly with everyone she met, and this quality kept Dorinda on her guard even during such routine activities as a walk in the park or a visit to a millinery shop.

Leaving her own bedchamber, Dorinda walked down the corridor to Letty's bedchamber and tapped lightly on the door. After a moment, she stepped into the room, then paused, taken aback when she noted that neither Letty nor her abigail was there. Earlier, Letty had begged off their customary late afternoon drive to Hyde Park on the grounds that she was tired and wanted to take a nap. Dorinda had not believed this excuse for a minute—Letty had boundless energy and was *never* tired—but London was still very thin of company, and their drives had been rather placid affairs during which they rarely encountered anyone they knew. Dorinda sensed that Letty had evaded today's drive out of sheer boredom, not fatigue. Peerless horsewoman that she was, Letty would much have preferred to ride, not drive, but she was prevented from doing so because Dorinda herself had never learned to ride.

Tapping her foot irritably as the moments passed, Dorinda was about to ring for a footman to inquire about Letty's whereabouts when the girl came bounding into the bedchamber, out of breath, her hair escaping in tousled curls from beneath an unbecoming mobcap. Looking askance at Letty's plain, ill-fitting kerseymere dress, which she did not recognize, Dorinda demanded, "Do you realize what time it is, Letty? And how in the world did you come by that dreadful gown?"

Letty's open face could rarely hide her thoughts. She looked distinctly uncomfortable as she replied airily, "Is it so very late, Dorinda? I'm sorry. I was out walking with Betsy. I'll hurry to dress for Grandmama's party."

Dorinda looked at her narrowly. "Out walking? Wearing that hideous cap and dress? Where could you go, dressed like that?" Dorinda's voice sharpened. "Letty! Out with it! You've been up to something."

Letty broke into a chuckle. "Well, yes, I suppose I was, but it was nothing so very bad, not really. Betsy and I went for a walk in the Green Park, and then—then we turned into St. James Street."

"St. James Street!" gasped Dorinda. "You know that was one of the first things Lady Torrington warned you about when we came to London: No lady who values her reputation will walk down St. James Street in the afternoon. Why did you do it?"

"I wanted to see the famous bow window at White's Club, where Mr. Brummell sits with his friends," replied Letty simply.

"Well, did you see Mr. Brummell?" asked Dorinda, feeling foolish but unable to contain her curiosity.

"I don't really know. There were only two men sitting in the bow window. One had paint all over his face, as if he were about to step out on a stage, and he wore a yellow satin suit. The other man was dressed in a bright green coat and pantaloons. If either of them was Mr. Brummell, I can't think why he has such a reputation for elegance." Letty giggled. "Lord, it was such a hum. Just as Betsy and I were passing the window, the man in the green coat lifted his quizzing glasses and stared at us, and for a moment I was in a panic, thinking how dreadful it would be if I were introduced to the man later in the season and he recognized me. But, of course, that's impossible. *Nobody* could recognize me in Betsy's mobcap and kerseymere dress, and I had Cook's old cloak bundled around me with the hood pulled half over my face."

"I daresay there isn't much likelihood that you've been recognized, but, Letty, whatever possessed you to do such a thing?"

A shadow crossed Letty's usually sunny face. "It's so dull and uneventful here a good deal of the time." She sighed. "I thought London would be much more exciting, but since we arrived we've spent most of our time shopping for clothes or leaving calling cards or visiting Grandmama's ancient friends—or viewing the pictures at the Royal Academy. Of course, I did like the Tower zoo and the balloon ascent at Vauxhall Gardens, but—" her voice grew wistful—"back home, it's shearing time, my favorite mare is due to foal next month, and I'd like to see the blooms on the new rose variety that our head gardener planted last autumn—"

"I think you'll find life much more interesting after the season really starts, Letty. Time will pass so quickly that you'll be back in the country before you know it. Hurry now, you haven't much time to dress."

Returning to Letty's bedchamber a little later, Dorinda found her charge transformed into an elfin charmer in a white crepe dress with long sleeves of delicate lace and a flounce embellished with pearl embroidery. Letty's cropped tawny curls, worn loose and dishevelled, were threaded with pearls. Dorinda complimented Letty on her appearance and then asked a bit nervously, "How do I . . . do I look all right?"

Letty gave her a quick hug. "You must know that you

look charming and stylishly elegant. Why would you doubt it?"

"Well, it's my first dinner party and I wouldn't want to disappoint Lady Torrington."

"Pooh. You look as though you were born to the Ton. Oh, I know what you're thinking about; Grandma doesn't want anybody to know that your mama was an actress. But *I* say, why should it matter? Actresses lead such interesting lives."

"Believe me, Letty, it wouldn't do for your grandmother's friends to know about my background. Are you ready to go down?"

As they walked out of the room, Letty said with a touch of discontent, "I do wish that Grandmama weren't having this dinner party. It will be so dull—mostly her friends, and all they will want to talk about are politics and scandals and cards. Too lowering." Then, brightening, she added, "One thing to the good, though. Cook tells me we're having strawberries tonight. She says that it's sinful what they cost—over a hundred and fifty pounds."

Shocked though she was at this instance of conspicuous consumption, Dorinda remembered to say, "You shouldn't spend so much time with Cook." Letty was still grinning at this automatic reproof as they entered the drawing room. The dowager, imposing in silver tissue with a matching turban, gave Dorinda a long searching look before saying, "You look very well, Miss Hayle. That gown suits you. Don't you agree, Fanny?" Her companion, Miss Minniott, murmured her usual uncritical assent. Dorinda sometimes thought that Lady Torrington employed the faded, elderly lady just to have someone to carry out her masterful will without ever talking back.

"I had hoped to have Shalford here tonight," Lady Torrington was saying, "but today I learned that he hasn't come to town yet. However, his sister-in-law, Lady Lionel

Leyburne, and her daughter arrived in London yesterday and will be here."

Clapping her hands, Letty exclaimed, "Oh, I'm so glad. It will be so pleasant to see Emily again."

Lady Torrington had spoken of giving a small dinner, but as Dorinda sat down to table it seemed to her that the meal was more like a banquet. The two courses consisted of every cut of meat and game and every variety of fish and poultry that she could think of; and in addition to a mouth-watering array of jellies, ices, trifles, sweetmeats, and Italian rusks, there was an enormous pyramid of hothouse fruits, including pineapples and the astonishingly expensive strawberries. Dorinda found that she had little to do except enjoy the excellent food and sit quietly while the cloud of unfamiliar gossip wafted gently around her. There was great interest around the table in the Prince Regent's friendship with a certain Lady Hertford and in the latest doings of the harum-scarum Lady Caroline Lamb, but the burning question of the day seemed to be the possibility that the Prince might call for a coalition government. Mention was made, too, of a recently published poem called *Childe Harold's Pilgrimage* by a hitherto obscure peer named Byron. The comments on this work so intrigued Dorinda that she vowed to herself she would read it. Poor Letty, to the close observer, was obviously as bored as she had predicted she would be, but she was suffering through the dinner table gossip with an admirable patience.

After dinner, leaving the gentlemen to their port, the ladies withdrew to the drawing room with its lofty coffered ceilings decorated with lovely cameo paintings. Lady Torrington, an inveterate card player, quickly formed a table for whist with Lady Lynnfield, Letty's godmother, and several other old cronies. Letty sat chatting vivaciously with Emily Leyburne, a shy and daintily beautiful girl with dark curls and china blue eyes.

"They like each other," smiled Lady Lionel Leyburne as she observed Dorinda gazing at the two girls. "They were both visiting at Bellwood last summer, Lord Lynnfield's estate, you know, and they took to each other instantly."

"What a good thing, since they will soon be related by marriage," said Dorinda without thinking. She paused, biting her lip. "I'm so sorry. I know I shouldn't have said that, the arrangement isn't generally known."

Lady Lionel was a quietly pretty, soft-spoken woman, a slightly worn version of her daughter. She smiled again as she said, "Pray don't refine on it, Miss Hayle. It's true, Shalford's engagement to Lady Letitia won't be announced, either officially or unofficially until well into the autumn. But I'm sure that my brother-in-law and Lady Torrington don't expect us in the family circle to avoid any mention of the marriage. In fact, I'm glad to have the opportunity to talk to you about it. I'm quite delighted with the news, and I've had nobody to share it with! Actually, I had begun to think that Justin might never marry at all—he's approaching his thirty-seventh birthday, you know—and then when I learned that he planned to marry this delightful girl, so spirited, so full of life . . . well, I can't tell you how pleased I was to hear it."

"Oh," said Dorinda a little blankly. "I hadn't realized that the duke was considerably older than Letty." She broke off, wondering if she were fated to get off on the wrong foot with Lady Lionel.

"You think that Letitia might be a little young for Justin? I confess, the thought has crossed my mind—but there, I'm sure it's of no consequence. My husband and I were both just eighteen when we married—you did know that Lionel and Justin were twins?—and I sometimes think that it might have been better if Lionel had been a little older and more mature than I."

"No, I wasn't aware that the duke and your husband were twins. Is Lord Lionel? . . ."

"Dead these many years, my dear," said Lady Lionel wistfully. "Not long after my children were born. I've always had a fancy that his brother's early death was responsible for keeping Justin a bachelor for so long. Because, you see, Lionel's children were twins also—Emily and Edmund—and Justin simply took us over as his family. Lionel didn't leave us very prosperous, so we've always lived with Justin. He's been very good to us, providing for Edmund's education and for Emily's dowry. I believe Justin came to think of Edmund as his own son, rather than just his legal heir. So then, last year, when . . ." Lady Lionel fumbled for a handkerchief, brushing away a tear from each eye. "Last year we lost Edmund. He broke his neck in a stupid accident, racing the curricle that he had just received from his uncle as a birthday gift."

"I'm so sorry. What a tragedy for all of you."

"Thank you, my dear. I didn't mean to distress you. We've all learned to cope pretty well, most of the time. For Justin, of course, Edmund's death meant that he had to think of the succession. The next heir is a childless old man, a very distant cousin. And so, since Justin had to marry in any event, I'm so happy that he's marrying for love."

From her seat in a private box on the third tier, Dorinda looked around the vast interior of the theatre with a sense of awed unreality. Just as Lady Torrington's small dinner party two days ago had been her first introduction to society, so this performance tonight at Covent Garden would mark her first public appearance as Letty's companion.

Compared to the little New Road Theatre in Brighton, Covent Garden was a leviathan. There were two galleries and three tiers of boxes, the third tier consisting of twenty-three private boxes, each with its own anteroom. There was a roomy pit with two central aisles, before which was an enormous stage. Above were large numbers of glass chandeliers, forty of them, according to Lady Lynnfield, Letty's godmother, whose box they were sharing. Lady Lynnfield had also told Dorinda that the theatre could hold as many as three thousand patrons.

Dorinda had been looking forward with immense anticipation to this performance of *Othello*. The redoubtable John Kemble was in the lead role and his equally famous sister, Sarah Siddons, was making one of her rare recent appearances as Desdemona. However, Dorinda's pleasure was very nearly doused at the outset when, leaning over the railing of the box before the curtain rose to glance around the audience, she spotted the supercilious hawklike features of Sir Fabian Mordaunt in the second tier of boxes. Her heart beating faster, she pushed her chair away from the railing. How could she have been so naive? In accepting Lady Torrington's offer of a position, it had never entered her mind that she might encounter in London so well-known a figure as the Prince Regent's equerry. Well, she thought to herself grimly, what will be, will be. Moreover there was a good chance, even if she met Sir Fabian face to face, that he might not recognize her without her stage paint, costume, and wig. She pushed him to the back of her mind and forced herself to concentrate on the play.

Her eyes were so intent on the stately Kemble's first entrance that she was paying little attention to the other actors on stage, and it was a minor shock, therefore, to hear Letty's suppressed squeal of delight in the second scene of the first act: "Dorinda! Isn't that . . . yes it *is*. It's Mr. Barry, the man who—"

Startled, Dorinda shot a nervous glance at Lady Lynnfield, and then had the presence of mind to whisper urgently to Letty, "Shush, remember that your grandmother doesn't want us to talk about my connection with the theatre."

Turning her eyes back to the stage, she saw that Letty was correct: There, dressed like Kemble in baggy breeches, long dressing-gownlike coat and plumed turban, was Desmond Barry, addressing Othello in Cassio's first speech, " 'The duke does greet you, general; And he requires your haste-post-haste appearance Even on the instant.' "

Desmond walked now without a trace of his limp, and Dorinda was so bemused at seeing a friend actually playing on the famous stage that it came as an anticlimax when she observed Cassandra Bell in a nonspeaking part among Desdemona's ladies. Nor was her disappointment as sharp as it might have been when she realized why the majestic Siddons was appearing so rarely these days at Covent Garden: Sarah Siddons was now immensely fat and showed every year of her age.

At the interval, Letty was murmuring excitedly, "Mr. Barry spotted us up here, Dorinda—he *winked* at me, did you notice?" when a theatre attendant entered the box and handed Dorinda a note. "Now, who on earth could be writing to you, Miss Hayle," began Lady Lynnfield before she was distracted by the first arrival of a stream of visitors to the box, all of whom had to be introduced to her goddaughter and her companion.

Quickly whisking the note into her reticule, Dorinda concentrated on remembering the names and faces of Lady Lynnfield's friends, who, judging by their numbers, seemed to include most of the notables present in the theatre. She suppressed a pang of fear, steeling herself to be calm, when Sir Fabian appeared at the door of the box. But the equerry flicked only a careless glance at Dorinda in her becoming but conservatively cut gown of dark blue sarsenet. He immediately fixed his eyes on Letty, radiant in gossamer white gauze and lace, even as he bowed to Lady Lynnfield. Dorinda noted with some satisfaction that he was still moving his right arm and shoulder rather gingerly.

"Good evening, Sir Fabian. How kind of you to call," said Lady Lynnfield with what seemed a certain lack of cordiality. "How is His Royal Highness? In good health, I trust?"

"Oh, pretty stout, ma'am. He sometimes has a sort of numbing ache in his arm, but, as you well know, he never allows the state of his health to interfere with the performance of his duties. Will you do me the honor of introducing me to your goddaughter?"

Lady Lynnfield included Dorinda in the introductions, but Sir Fabian, addressing the sketchiest of bows to Dorinda, lavished his full attention on Letty. After he had left, Lady Lynnfield leaned over to Dorinda and said in a low voice, "I think I must warn you about Sir Fabian, Miss Hayle. He comes from a good family, of course, and he's the regent's equerry, but I should not allow him, if I were you, to spend much time in Letitia's company. He has a reputation for wildness and for being a gazetted fortune hunter. The *on-dit* is that he will soon be in Dun territory unless he marries a wealthy wife. I daresay that he could tell you almost to the penny the size of Letitia's fortune."

She broke off to greet a newcomer to the box, a tall, broadshouldered man with dark curls fashionably arranged "à la Titus," lazy hazel eyes, and classically chiseled features. His coat of black superfine, his white silk breeches, and his white marcella waistcoat fit without a wrinkle, as if they were part of his own skin, but without any suggestion of too tight a fit. Feeling as if the theatre were about to collapse around her, Dorinda heard Lady Lynnfield exclaim, "My dear Justin, what a pleasant surprise. Honoria Torrington was saying just the other evening that you weren't expected in town for some days yet."

"Fortunately, I was able to finish up my estate business sooner than I had expected. But let me introduce myself . . . Miss Hayle, I believe? Lady Torrington has told me about you. I'm Shalford." Pausing slightly, the duke gazed intently at Dorinda. "I have the oddest notion . . . Have we met before, Miss Hayle?"

Dorinda forced her features into polite immobility. "I hardly think so, Your Grace. This is my first visit to London."

As Shalford, his forehead still furrowed in vague perplexity, turned away to sit beside Letty, Dorinda slowly exhaled a sigh of relief. But her sense of respite was only momentary, as she reflected on her situation. What a monstrous piece of bad luck, how fiendishly coincidental that both Sir Fabian Mordaunt and Letty's future husband had seen her on stage during her pitifully brief career, and that both of them had been on the receiving end of her chastising hand. Either or both of them, in recognizing her as Rachel Conroy, erstwhile actress, could blast her future and that of her mother merely by revealing her theatrical connection to the dowager. To a great extent she might be able to avoid Sir Fabian, but Shalford! Was it realistic to hope that he could be in her company continually over the next few months without recognizing her as Rachel Conroy?

Once again Dorinda tamped down her fears, willing herself into calmness. She watched Shalford was he sat talking to Letty, and was amazed to see that the girl, usually so vivacious and talkative, was behaving like a shy-voiced schoolgirl. Was it possible that Letty was in awe of this older, vastly more sophisticated man who wanted to marry her?

"Are you enjoying the play, Lady Letitia?" asked the duke.

"Oh, yes, very much," responded Letty primly. Then, her normal frankness surfacing, she added, "Well, it might be just a trifle dull in spots, you know. Now the other night Dorinda and I saw a *really* exciting play at Drury Lane." Letty shivered enjoyably, and her mobile little face came alive as she described to Shalford the scene in *One O'clock*,

by Matthew Lewis, in which the fearsome tyrant
Hardiknute is dragged by a demon into a cavern and men-
aced by flames of blue fire issuing from the mouths of
writhing serpents. "Mr. Lewis also wrote *The Monk*," she
informed the duke. "Have you read it?"

Shalford threw back his head and laughed. "Have I not! I
had just entered Cambridge, and was feeling very grown-up
indeed, but after reading that book I had nightmares for a
week's running."

After this admission, some of Letty's shyness seemed to
evaporate, and the duke remained beside her for a few
minutes longer, drawing her out and listening to her artless
prattle while an appreciative, amused little smile wreathed
his lips. When another of Lady Lynnfield's acquaintances
entered the box to be introduced to Letty, Shalford left his
chair beside her and came over to sit down next to Dorinda.

"I believe Lady Torrington told me that you come from
Northumberland, Miss Hayle," he said, as if making casual
conversation. But Dorinda, already apprehensive about
overly close contact with him, had the distinct impression
that, behind those languid eyes of his, there was more than
polite disinterest. "I trust you had a pleasant journey to
London."

"Indeed, yes. Lady Torrington kindly saw to that."
Thankful that she had had the foresight to read about
Northumberland in a guidebook, Dorinda was able to fill up
the next few moments of conversation with utterly spurious
details of her journey from the north of England.

Again an intent, rather perplexed look crossed Shalford's
face. "Northumberland," he mused. "I was up there a few
years ago, visiting the Duke at Alnwick. Isn't it possible . . .
are you sure that we never met at that time?"

"Quite sure," declared Dorinda firmly. "My family home
is a tiny village near Otterburn, not far from the Cheviots,
but a considerable distance from Alnwick." She added inno-

cently, "I can assure you, if my family and I had had the honor of meeting the Duke of Shalford, we would certainly not have forgotten it!"

Shalford gave her a quick, hard glance, as if he did not quite know how to take her last remark. Then, relaxing, he said, "Do you think that you will like living here, Miss Hayle? Are you fond of the theatre?"

Dorinda swallowed hard. Was this a loaded question? Had the duke begun to make the connection between Dorinda Hayle and Rachel Conroy? Crossing her fingers beneath her reticule, she replied, "Oh, yes. I especially love Shakespeare, and I was so looking forward to seeing *Othello* tonight. . . ." A look of surprise appeared on her face as a vague thought that had been hovering at the back of her mind crystallized into consciousness.

"Yes, Miss Hayle?"

"Well, I know that Mr. Kemble is considered our greatest English actor," began Dorinda slowly, almost forgetting the presence of her companion. "But somehow, I found him very . . . very artificial, very mannered. I did not care for his statuesque poses and his rather singsong way of speaking."

Raising an eyebrow, Shalford replied with a quick interest. "I quite agree with you. I think that the so-called classical style of acting may have run its course. I saw a young actor a few years ago in Ireland—I believe his name was Kean, yes, that was it, Edmund Kean—who played Barabbas in *The Jew of Malta* with such passion, such realism, that I left the theatre feeling almost as though I had met the devil in person."

His manner changing, he said abruptly, "I've been wanting to talk to you for some time. We needn't go into it deeply but I know that you're aware of my . . . my hopes for Lady Letitia. I think it an excellent idea that she is to have a sensible, well-bred young woman as her companion during this coming season. Lady Torrington is old now, and not too

well, and I think she finds it hard to relate to someone of
Letty's generation. So I am depending on you, Miss Hayle,
to guide Letty, to give her the benefit of an older, wiser
head. In some ways she's very young for her age, overly
friendly, overly trusting. These qualities, in a young girl of
her rank and fortune, may well inspire some individuals,
among the host of new acquaintances that she will be
making, to attempt to take advantage of her good nature.
But I won't belabor the point. I'm sure that you know very
well what I mean."

Dorinda bowed her head, saying quietly, "I understand
very well, Your Grace. I will certainly do my best to live up
to Lady Torrington's trust."

"Excellent. I can leave the matter, then, in your very
capable hands. It was pleasant talking with you. Good
night."

As the duke left the box, Dorinda gazed after him with a
calm expression that masked an inward fury. Beneath
Shalford's smiling condescending courtesy, she had felt the
steely arrogance of his unspoken command: She was to erect
a protective barrier around Letty, warding off unwelcome
suitors and delivering her charge into the ducal arms at the
end of the season. And what had he called her? An older
and wiser head? Unwillingly, Dorinda found herself remembering that evening at the New Road Theatre in Brighton,
when she had stood locked in the passionate arms of a dark
stranger. Had he thought of her as older and wiser then? she
wondered resentfully. For a moment she would have been
happy to throw up her position as Letty's chaperon in return
for the opportunity to castigate this careless, uncaring roué
with a blistering opinion of his behavior. How grossly unfair
that he should feel free to attempt the seduction of any
woman of inferior birth who crossed his path, while at the
same time requiring that a very young girl come to him
virginal and untouched.

The last of the visitors had left the box as the orchestra struck up the music for the harlequinade, and Dorinda, giving her head a little shake, smiled wryly at herself. What a total waste of energy it was to question a double standard that had, doubtless, been in effect since the Flood! Seeking to banish Shalford from her thoughts, she began surreptitiously to examine the note that had been delivered to her earlier. As she had half expected, it was from Desmond Barry.

"My dearest, darling girl," he wrote, "what a delightful surprise to see you in the theatre tonight. Do you have the second sight, I wonder? Did some instinct tell you to attend this performance? If you had come to Covent Garden on any other night you might have missed me in the crowd; but today the actor who regularly plays Cassio came down sick, so Kemble gave me my first big chance. And did you notice Cassie among Desdemona's ladies?

"My darling Dorinda, I've never seen you look more beautiful. London life obviously agrees with you! I must see you soon. Never fear, I won't call on you at Lady Torrington's house. Just send a message around to the theatre telling me where we can meet. How about the Green Park?"

Dorinda felt a warm rush of pleasure at Desmond's affectionate note, but she instantly realized that their friendship could have no future as long as she remained in Lady Torrington's employ. The dowager would never countenance an actor as a hanger-on in her granddaughter's circle.

Chapter V

"You know, Dorinda, I do think that all this business of paying calls and leaving cards is deadly dull," observed Letty discontentedly as their carriage rolled past the fashionable shops along Bond Street. "What purpose does it really serve?"

Privately, Dorinda rather agreed with her charge, but she replied sensibly, "It's just the way things are in society, my dear, and there is nothing we can do about it. And you must admit that not all your calls are dull. This afternoon, for example, you'll be seeing Emily Leyburne, and you're always saying that you never have the opportunity for a really cozy chat with her."

Letty brightened. "That's true. Even when we attend the same party in the evening, we usually catch only the briefest glimpse of each other."

The carriage crossed Oxford Street, made the turning into Henrietta Place, and halted before the stately bulk of Leyburne House in Cavendish Square. As she followed

Letty to the door, Dorinda suppressed as unrealistic a fugitive hope that she would not encounter the Duke of Shalford in his own drawing room. It was now several days since she had made the appalling discovery that the obnoxious Corinthian who had forced his attentions on her at the theatre in Brighton was actually Letty's future husband. She had not seen him since their meeting at Covent Garden, but it was inevitable that their paths would cross early and often. She had best learn to live with the constant tension and the fear that at any moment she might be exposed.

As it turned out, though Lady Lionel's rooms were comfortably full, her brother-in-law was not among those present. To Dorinda's discomfort, however, Sir Fabian Mordaunt was there, and he crossed the drawing room to talk to Letty the instant that he spotted her arrival. However, as at Covent Garden, his eye passed unseeingly over the unimportant figure of Letty's companion. After a smiling five minutes devoted to bestowing on Letty a string of admiring compliments, he moved on to speak to Lady Lionel.

"I don't like that man," murmured Letty. "He does look at one so. I suspect that he's a loose screw."

"Letty! You shouldn't say such things."

"Such fustian! You surely don't want me to be a Friday-faced hypocrite!" Letty's gamin smile faded as she watched Sir Fabian with Lady Lionel. "I daresay it's just a take-in, but I heard the other day that Sir Fabian and Emily's mama were once very much in love. But she didn't have a large fortune and he had gambled away *his*, so nothing came of it and she married Lord Lionel."

"Someone must have been telling you a whisker," said Dorinda firmly, finding it impossible to believe that the sweetly gracious Lady Lionel had ever entertained a tender emotion for anyone as obnoxious as Sir Fabian.

But Letty was not attending. "Perry!" she squealed, raising her hand to wave vigorously at the tall, gangling young man who had just entered the room. He came over immediately, his bright blue eyes dancing beneath a crop of crisp chestnut curls.

"Well, by George, I heard that you were in town," he exclaimed. He eyed Letty critically. "I'm dashed if you haven't improved beyond all knowing since I saw you at Christmas. You're halfway presentable now, my girl."

"Please, Perry, stop trying to turn me up sweet. You'll make me blush with your compliments," grinned Letty. "Dorinda, this is Peregrine Lacey. His family live near us in Leicestershire. Perry, this is Miss Hayle, my new companion. Only you're not to treat her like a companion, mind. She's my friend."

"Your servant, Miss Hayle."

"Perry, your mama told me just before I left for London that you were expecting your commission in the First Life Guards to come through at any moment."

"Which it did, just three weeks ago. Cornet Lacey, at your service."

"What wonderful news." Letty beamed. "I can't wait to see you in your new regimentals."

"Lord, there's nothing to that. Come see us Sunday at the Horse Guards Parade in Whitehall. Though it's such a waste of time, really," Perry added disconsolately. "I thought when I joined up that I'd soon see some fighting. I can't imagine why the Duke of Wellington hasn't sent for the Household Cavalry now that he's taken Ciudad Rodrigo and the way to Madrid is open. But no, he's using the Fifth Dragoon Guards and the Light Dragoons."

"Well, Perry, I'm jolly glad that you aren't in the Peninsula," interrupted Letty. "I'd much rather see your familiar face here in London while I'm doing the season." She paused to gaze at the small flat hat that he held in his hand, and at the large blue-spotted handkerchief that he had

knotted around his shirt points in place of a cravat. "Why
are you wearing that peculiar hat, and what is that spotted
thing around your neck?"

"By Jove, Letty, don't you know anything?" demanded
Perry indignantly. "This hat is all the crack, let me tell you.
As for the neckerchief—well, Jem Belcher wears one like
this all the time."

"Who's Jem Belcher?"

Perry threw up his hands. "I wouldn't have believed it.
You've never heard of the Champion of England?"

"I don't think that females in general know very much
about the sport of prizefighting, Mr. Lacey." Dorinda
smiled, thinking that Perry and Letty were speaking to each
other not as a young man and a young woman, but as two
boys would, or as the childhood playmates they undoubtedly
had been.

"Do you still have the matched bays that you received on
your eighteenth birthday, Perry?" asked Letty.

Perry's eyes kindled. "Oh, rather. And you should see the
high-perch phaeton that I bought when my godfather gave
me a bit of the ready at Christmastime. I'm having it
brought up to London." To Dorinda, he explained,
"M'godfather's rich as a nabob—well, he *is* a nabob, for
that matter—and occasionally he can be persuaded to lay
out a little blunt."

Perry's eyes wandered across the room to where Sir
Fabian sat chatting with Emily Leyburne. "Look at that,"
he said disapprovingly. "Mordaunt's a million years too old
for Miss Leyburne and I hear that he's none to plump in the
pocket, so why is he dangling after her? Everybody knows
that she's no heiress, even if she *is* the niece of the Duke of
Shalford, and the *on-dit* is that Mordaunt has to marry
money. I will say this for him, though," Perry finished
handsomely, "he's a first-rate fiddler, drives to the inch.
He's a member of the Four-in-Hand Club, you know. My

eye and Betty Martin, what I'd give to be nominated to that—"

"Oh, I don't think that Emily would be interested in somebody as old as Sir Fabian," said Letty. "She's so pretty, I'm sure that she will have scores of eligible admirers." Her eyes dancing, Letty added teasingly, "Including you, Perry? I was wondering why you were spending a free afternoon paying calls. It's not a bit like you."

"Well, whyever not?" demanded Perry, reddening. "Miss Leyburne's the prettiest girl in London, and I have as much right as anyone, I suppose, to pay my court to her. Of course," he added gloomily, "her uncle will probably send me packing, because I'm a younger son with no expectations unless my godfather leaves me all his money—which ain't likely, because I'm not his only godchild."

"Well, Dorinda, I certainly expected that you would emerge from Hatchard's with an armful of books after spending all that time in the shop," observed Letty, a twinkle in her eyes as she gazed at the lone volume in Dorinda's hand. They were standing on the pavement outside Hatchard's book shop in Piccadilly Street, where Dorinda had been browsing blissfully for more than an hour.

"Oh, Letty, I'm sorry," said Dorinda contritely. "It must have been a dead bore for you, waiting for me to make my selection. It's just that I've never been in such a well-stocked shop before." And it had been a very long time, too, she thought, since she had allowed herself the luxury of buying a book or, indeed, anything else of a personal nature that was not an absolute necessity.

"Lady Letitia, Miss Hayle, an unexpected pleasure."

It was the first time that Dorinda had met the duke since their encounter at Covent Garden, and she viewed his tall, elegant figure with considerable trepidation, wondering if the sight of her in the bright sunshine of a May morning would nudge his slumbering memory. However, though his bow to her was more than perfunctorily polite, all his attention was centered on Letty, whose elfin face blushed slightly and whose smile held a trace of the same shyness toward Shalford that Dorinda had noted at their meeting at Covent Garden.

"I was just coming from Manton's shooting gallery when I saw you leaving Hatchard's," remarked Shalford.

"Are you a good shot?" asked Letty, her eyes lighting up. "How I should like to go to Manton's to cup a wafer! It really doesn't seem fair that so many of the most interesting places in London are barred to females!"

"And what, pray, would you do at Manton's?" smiled Shalford. "Don't tell me that you can handle a pistol!"

"Oh, can I not? And not just pistols, either. Last summer my brother Richard taught me to use a gun. One day—it was such a lark—I put on a suit of his old clothes and went out after pigeons with him. And would you believe it? I came home with a nice brace of wood pigeons and Richard didn't get any. Only the butler spied me entering the house, still in Richard's clothes, and what a time I had, persuading him not to tell Grandmama! Oh!" Letty paused in comic dismay.

Shalford burst into laughter. "Don't worry, Lady Letitia. I shan't tell Lady Torrington, either." He turned to Dorinda. "I see that you found something to interest you in Hatchard's. May I?"

Shalford took the book that Dorinda handed to him and leafed briefly through the pages, pausing to quote softly, " 'Adieu, adieu! my native shore Fades o'er the waters blue; The night-winds sigh, the breakers roar, And shrieks the wild sea-mew.' " He gave the book back to Dorinda, saying, "I'm sure that you will enjoy *Childe Harold*, Miss Hayle. Whatever else he might be, the man's a poet."

"Do you know Lord Byron, Duke?"

"Oh, yes, slightly at least. The man's taking London by storm, you know. As a matter of fact, I was just in Byron's company. We were having a little target competition at Manton's."

"Who won?" inquired Letty with an impudent little grin.

"I did, naturally." Shalford raised an eyebrow in mock hauteur. "Well, just barely. Byron can shoot too. Where are you ladies going? May I escort you somewhere? My curricle is down the street. I think that we could all of us squeeze in."

Dorinda glanced at Letty. "We were on our way to the Royal Academy. If you would care to accompany us? . . ."

"With pleasure. You're an art lover then, Lady Letitia?" Shalford cocked a teasing eye at Letty. "Or perhaps . . . might I suggest that you postpone your visit to Somerset House and come with me to a balloon ascension in Hyde Park?"

"Oh, yes, please. I *love* balloon ascensions." Letty was ecstatic. "We can see all those dull old pictures some other time—oops, sorry, Dorinda, I know that you like those dull old—oh, dear, my wretched tongue!"

"Don't refine on it, Letty." Dorinda smiled. "The paintings will certainly be at Somerset House for the rest of the season, but who knows when there will be another balloon ascension?"

She was rewarded by a delighted smile from Letty and a quietly approving nod from Shalford. In the end, it was decided that the duke's curricle would be a tight fit for the three of them, so Dorinda and Letty, in the Wingate barouche, followed along behind Shalford to the roped-off enclosure in Hyde Park where a number of carriages were already drawn up, their occupants watching the workmen bring up the casks of hydrogen that would inflate the bag of the balloon. After expertly guiding the curricle to a spot alongside the Wingate carriage, Shalford climbed down to stand beside the barouche.

"There isn't much wind today," he commented. "Perhaps the flight will have to be postponed, unless they're counting on stronger air currents as the balloon rises."

"Don't even think about a postponement," begged Letty. "No, see, they're about to attach the hose pipe."

Soon the silken folds of the bag, which had been lying limply on the ground, stirred gently as the hydrogen gas flowed into the bag. In a few minutes the bag swelled and filled and began to tug against the enveloping netting that was attached to a metal hoop from which was suspended, also by netting, the gaily painted car. The aeronauts piled into the car, the mooring ropes were cast off, and the enormous green-and-white-striped sphere mounted gracefully into the sky.

"Ooh . . . I can't see that balloon anymore because of the trees behind us," breathed a disappointed Letty. "I think I'll just jump out and run into the meadow over there."

Before Dorinda could remonstrate, Letty had descended nimbly from the barouche and was running lightly over the grass of the adjoining meadow, where she joined a group of boys and young men in the center of the area. Dorinda glanced apprehensively at Shalford, but his eyes were fixed on Letty as she stood craning her neck for a last look at the rapidly disappearing balloon.

A tender, rueful little smile wreathing his lips, Shalford murmured, "She really hasn't grown up yet, has she? Sometimes she's . . . not childish, exactly, but—"

"No, not childish, Your Grace. Childlike, perhaps. Letty has the gift of savoring each moment to the full," said Dorinda quietly.

"Look over there, Dorinda. That lady you were asking

about the other day—I think I know who she is. It's Harriette Wilson."

Seated with Letty in the Wingate barouche for their daily drive in Hyde Park, Dorinda gazed with considerable interest at the red-haired, somewhat plump young woman who sat by the side of the road in a carriage lined with pale blue satin. She was surrounded by a horde of eager horsemen, each of them intent on snatching a word with the reigning beauty among this season's "Fashionable Impures"—except that Miss Wilson was not really a beauty, Dorinda reflected, as the Wingate carriage drove past that of the popular courtesan. Obviously she must have charms that escaped the eye of the casual beholder!

"I hear that Lord Worcester—the Duke of Beaufort's heir, you know—was so much in love with Harriette Wilson that he actually wanted to marry her," observed Letty. "His papa had to buy him a commission and whisk him off to serve with the Duke of Wellington in the Peninsula."

"You shouldn't be talking of such things," reproved the mildly scandalized Dorinda.

"I don't see why not. I heard Grandmama talking about it."

Letty's statement only confirmed a suspicion that had been growing in Dorinda's mind for some time: For all her concern that Letty's impulsive, unconventional personality might get her into trouble, Lady Torrington herself came from a much more earthy, outspoken generation. There was the dowager's crony, Lady Melbourne, for instance—young Caroline Lamb's mother-in-law—whose six children reputedly all had different fathers, and whose social status remained beyond challenge because her love affairs had been conducted with suitable discretion.

It was five o'clock of a lovely afternoon in late May, and the season by now was in full swing. Letty had already attended so many parties that she recognized, and was recognized by, everyone who mattered in the *beau monde*. As Dorinda watched Letty wave to a girlish acquaintance here, bow to a matron there, or laughingly fend off a compliment from one of her ardent swains, it was hard to remember that the vivid face under the fetching gypsy hat of beribboned straw had slightly irregular features and was not really beautiful.

Letty waved the carriage to a halt as a barouche bearing Lady Lionel and Emily came into view from the opposite direction.

"I forgot to ask you, are you going to Countess Lieven's *fête champêtre* tomorrow?" Letty asked Emily.

"Oh, yes. It sounds so diverting. But, Letty, I must tell you what Mr. Elliot said about you last night at Almack's—he said that you were quite the most accomplished partner he had danced with this season!"

"Then he must be half blind, because it's obvious to everyone that, compared to you, I have all the grace of a . . . a camel!" retorted Letty.

While Emily, her pretty face suffused with a blush, was saying in distress, "That's just not true. You're an accomplished dancer," Letty's mother smiled and said in a low voice to Dorinda, "It wouldn't matter, you know, if Lady Letitia danced with a wooden leg, nobody would notice. She has a gift for captivating people. I can quite see why Shalford lost his heart to her the very moment that he first saw her."

Lady Lionel and Emily had no sooner driven on when Desmond Barry came alongside the Wingate carriage, riding a livery-stable hack.

Beaming, Letty exclaimed, "I'm so glad to see you. I've been wanting to tell you how much I enjoyed your perf—oh!" She stopped guiltily as Dorinda, casting a quick look around her, dug a warning elbow into Letty's ribs. "I've been wanting to tell you how much I enjoyed driving with you in Brighton," Letty finished primly.

"Oh, yes, Lady Letitia. I can see why driving with me would be a memorable occasion for you, especially considering the quality of my horses." Desmond laughed, casting a deprecating glance at his sorry steed as he dismounted.

As Desmond continued to chat with Letty, it provoked a trace of uneasiness in Dorinda to note that Letty was responding to his bantering, slightly rakish charm with rather more enthusiasm than Dorinda cared to see. It was therefore with some relief that she observed Peregrine Lacey driving a towering high-perch phaeton with yellow wings toward them.

Desmond was forgotten on the instant. "Oh-h-h, Perry, what a beauty," breathed Letty.

Giving the reins to his groom, Perry climbed down from his precarious driving perch. "Yes, I daresay you could call it a spanking turn-out," he admitted complacently. "Did you ever see two more elegant bits of blood than those bays?"

"No, never. Now there, Mr. Barry, is the kind of horseflesh that you should be riding. Oh, I'm sorry. Mr. Barry, this is my friend, Peregrine Lacey. Perry, Mr. Desmond Barry."

"Delighted, sir." Perry cast a dubious eye at Desmond's horse. "Er . . . you've just arrived in town, Mr. Barry?"

Catching Dorinda's anxious glance, Desmond smiled, saying, "Why yes, I've come from Ireland."

"Oh, Ireland." Perry waved a relieved hand. "You'll be bringing over your own horses then."

Desmond smiled again. "As soon as I can, yes."

"Care to come for a drive, Letty?" asked Perry. "Would that be all right, Miss Hayle? Or perhaps you'd like to try out the phaeton yourself?"

"No, indeed." Dorinda shivered as she peered up into the

driver's seat. "I value my neck too much. I'm not sure, Letty, that you should be riding in that thing, either. It doesn't look like a lady's vehicle to me."

"Oh, Dorinda, don't be such a spoilsport," wailed Letty, and Perry, an injured look replacing his usual sunny expression, exclaimed, "Next you'll be implying that I can't handle the ribbons."

"Mr. Lacey has a point there, Miss Hayle," grinned Desmond. "If he can navigate this phaeton through the crowded London streets, surely you can trust him to drive Lady Letitia around Hyde Park."

"Well, I suppose that it will be all right," Dorinda began doubtfully, but before she could finish her remark Letty had joyfully bolted out of the barouche and, displacing Perry's groom, was being helped into the phaeton.

"Now, why did you have to go and encourage Letty?" demanded Dorinda as she watched the phaeton disappear around the bend of the road.

"That little minx doesn't need encouraging," said an unrepentant Desmond. "I'd say that she was ripe for any spree."

"Exactly so," retorted Dorinda. "And now I think of it, how could you tell Peregrine Lacey that whopping lie about bringing over your horses from Ireland?"

"*He* said it. I just agreed with him. Well, you wouldn't have wanted me to tell him that the only horses I own are used to pull the waggons transporting my touring company scenery from town to town, now would you? But seriously, my dear, I thought that it would be an excellent idea to get rid of both Letty and her friend Lacey so that we could have a private talk. I've been waiting and waiting for a word from you, a note, even a line, so I finally decided today that the only way to get in contact with you was to search for you in Hyde Park. I was sure that you and Lady Letitia would be driving here on such a fine day."

"But I did write to you, Desmond, the very next day after I received the note that you sent to me during your performance in *Othello*. And I'm sure that the letter must have reached you, because—"

"Oh, *that* letter. The one saying that we couldn't meet, couldn't see each other," interrupted Desmond. "Yes, I received it. You know that I did, because I referred to its contents in the several letters that I've written to you since then. Letters to which you never saw fit to send me a reply."

"I didn't think it was necessary," replied Dorinda, biting her lip. "I'd said all that there was to say. Desmond, why can't you understand that it's impossible for you and me to have any friendly contact as long as I remain in Lady Torrington's employ? You know how important this position is to me. Mama's entire future depends on it."

"Of course I understand that Lady Torrington wouldn't countenance any open friendship between us, Dorinda. I know as well as you do that actors and aristocrats don't mix with each other socially. My God, up until a few years ago the acting profession was so disreputable that the greatest actress in France was refused burial in consecrated ground. Even today, let's admit it, most actresses are considered little better than common harlots—well, you had a taste of that yourself in Brighton, warding off that fellow Sir Fabian Mordaunt—so I don't expect you to invite me for tea, or to stand up to me at Almack's. I know; they wouldn't let me show my face inside the place. But couldn't we meet occasionally for a walk in the park, perhaps early in the morning so that no one would see us? Or you might even come to see me in my rooms. No, don't shake your head. I swear to you, I wouldn't try to take any advantage of you. The fact is, darling Dorinda, that I love you. I want to marry you."

As he spoke, his voice vibrant with emotion, Desmond had moved closer to the carriage. Now he reached over, attempting to take Dorinda's hand. She moved away slightly on the seat, holding her arms close to her body.

"I'm sorry, Desmond. I'm very fond of you. I wish that we could see each other—I feel very lonely here sometimes, like a fish out of water—but I can't risk it. I'm afraid that Lady Torrington would discharge me if she discovered that you and I were meeting secretly."

Desmond stared at her. "Are you really so afraid of Lady Torrington? Or is it that I'm not good enough to be your friend, let alone your lover, now that you've been hobnobbing with the swells?"

"No, of course that's not true."

"I'm not so sure. I think that I should do as you so obviously wish me to do, and stay away from you. I won't bother you again." Tight-lipped, Desmond tipped his hat to her and mounted his horse.

Feeling miserable, Dorinda stared after Desmond's retreating back. She knew that she had hurt him, but she failed to see what else she could have done. Despite the cost to her friendship with Desmond or to any deeper relationship with him, she could not put Charlotte Wingate's life-long security in jeopardy.

"Good afternoon, Miss Hayle. You're driving alone today. I trust that Lady Letitia is not unwell?"

As the Duke of Shalford reined in his horse beside the carriage, Dorinda was glad for once to see him. He provided a temporary distraction from the memory of the hurt in Desmond's eyes. She had, of course, met Shalford frequently during these past few weeks, always with a tinge of nervousness, a hint of danger because he might at any moment recall when and where they had first met. As she looked at him now, so elegant in his perfectly tailored coat, creaseless pantaloons, and brilliantly polished Hessians, she wondered again if he and Letty could really make a successful match of it. This enormously self-assured, fashionable man in his late thirties, who for all his exquisite manners and active social life often seemed to have boredom lurking at the back of his eyes, was obliged to marry for the sake of an heir. That being the case, he had found himself attracted to this ebullient, mercurial girl, who often seemed even younger than her years, perhaps just because she was so different from the typically demure, insipid young woman who was being offered on the marriage mart. Dorinda also questioned whether, during the course of the brief London season, Letty and Shalford could go much beyond acquiring a mere surface knowledge of each other. Shalford had tied his own hands by insisting that their betrothal should be kept a secret; even though he made it a point to attend every gathering to which he and Letty had been invited, he could never spend more than a few public moments with her as her unacknowledged suitor among a swarm of other suitors.

"Good afternoon, Your Grace. No, Letty isn't ill. We met Mr. Lacey soon after we entered the park, and she accepted his invitation to go driving in his new phaeton."

"Lacey? Isn't that the young Pink who's been dangling after my niece Emily? Or has he now transferred his attentions to Lady Letitia?"

The obvious displeasure in Shalford's voice is undoubtedly prompted by simple jealousy, thought Dorinda, but it probably does not augur very well for poor Perry's courtship of Emily Leyburne.

"There's nothing at all romantic in Mr. Lacey's relationship with Letty," she said now, repressing her usual resentment at Shalford's occasional rebuke, either implied or unconscious, that she was not doing her best to keep Letty's many admirers at a distance. "They are just friends, childhood playmates. Mr. Lacey's father has an estate, Eversleigh Court, near Letty's home in Leicestershire. And the pair also has another bond—they're both horse mad."

His expression softening, Shalford replied ruefully, "Oh,

I know all about Letty's consuming interest in life. I suspect that I may be forced to enlarge the stables at Brinton Abbey to accommodate the horses that she'll undoubtedly persuade me to buy for her. Good God, what—"

At Shalford's strangled expression, the startled Dorinda turned her head to observe, careening toward them around the bend of the road, Peregrine Lacey's high-perch phaeton with Letty at the reins. As she tore past them, narrowly missing a barouche pulling in behind the Wingate carriage, Letty lifted her whip to them with a broad, delighted smile before disappearing around the next curve.

Ripping out a furious oath, Shalford turned on Dorinda. "What are you about, Miss Hayle, allowing Letty to drive a high-perch phaeton pell-mell through Hyde Park? Don't you realize that these vehicles are very unstable because of their high center of gravity and are therefore fairly dangerous for a man to drive, let alone a delicate girl? Letty could have been killed—she could still be killed, before that blithering idiot Lacey sees fit to bring her back to us."

Even as her quick temper kindled at Shalford's angry accusation, Dorinda remembered with a sick pang that Emily Leyburne's twin brother Edmund, Shalford's nephew and heir, had died just the previous year while racing his curricle, a vehicle, moreover, that had been a birthday gift from his uncle. Possibly Shalford felt that his gift had been responsible for Edmund's death. In any event, Dorinda could understand Shalford's obvious fear that Letty's reckless style of driving might be endangering her life.

"I'm sure that Letty will return safely," she said in an attempt to soothe Shalford. "I had no idea that she would take the reins. When they started out, Mr. Lacey was driving. But really, you know, she's an excellent whip. Perry—Mr. Lacey—says that she's at home to a peg behind a pair of horses."

"If—and I use the word prayerfully—if Letty comes to

no harm from this escapade, I would remind you that driving a high-perch phaeton in Hyde Park is scarcely the mark of a lady of quality," rejoined Shalford, his voice dangerously calm. "As a result of this prank she could be branded as fast, as a hoyden. I trust that you will remember this in future, and that you will approach your duties with somewhat more discretion."

"I can certainly promise you that Letty won't drive Mr. Lacey's phaeton again," said Dorinda evenly. "I do, however, feel a certain sympathy for her. To Letty, these sedate daily drives in Hyde Park are very dull. She would so much rather be astride a horse, putting her mount to a rousing gallop, but since I don't ride——"

"Let me also remind you that ladies don't gallop in Hyde Park, either. And why don't you ride, pray? What kind of upbringing have you had?"

Suddenly Dorinda's simmering resentment burst into fury. "I was reared in a household that couldn't afford saddle horses or private carriages or riding lessons," she snapped. "Not all of us, Duke, were born to wealth and opportunity, with servants to wait on us hand and foot, servants too meek to answer back to their betters when an arrogant employer berates them for something that isn't their fault."

"Well, I notice, Miss Hayle, that *you* at least are not too meek to answer back to your betters."

Dorinda glared at Shalford. "I beg your pardon, Your Grace. I should have watched my tongue. There is no need for bad manners on my part since you are giving me such an inspired lesson in the art!"

"Famous!" sneered Shalford, his dark eyes blazing with rage. "Here we have a companion who not only neglects her charge scandalously but who has no compunction about insulting her charge's future husband. I wonder what Lady

Torrington will say when I tell her about this performance of yours!"

"I'm confident that her ladyship will at least listen to my side of the story, which is more than you see fit to do!"

Later Dorinda was to wonder to what lengths her verbal abuse of Shalford might have gone if Letty and Perry had not arrived back just then.

Helped down from the phaeton by Perry's waiting groom, who, Dorinda realized with a suddenly sinking heart, had probably overheard at least part of her battle royal with Shalford, Letty approached the barouche with a glowing smile.

"What a lark! I can't remember when I've enjoyed myself so much," she exclaimed. "Do you own a high-perch phaeton, Duke?"

"I do not," he replied grimly. "I prefer not to make a cake of myself—nor do I endanger the lives of the young ladies of my acquaintance." He fixed Perry with a scathing eye. "Look here, Lacey: If you so much as allow my niece Emily to get within one foot of that obscene contraption you call a phaeton, I will forbid you the house. Good day, Lady Letitia, Miss Hayle. Good day to you, sir."

As she watched the duke ride off, Dorinda felt some of her own anger dissolve into a secret mirth. Once again Shalford's strategy of keeping his betrothal a secret had backfired against him. Since he had no official standing as Letty's fiancé, he had no authority to forbid her to drive Perry's phaeton, nor any right to be angry at Perry for allowing her to do so. Instead, he had struck out against the bewildered Perry, forbidding him to do something—to invite Emily Leyburne to ride in his phaeton—that undoubtedly had never even occurred to the young Guards officer.

Chapter VI

Dorinda peered into the mirror to give her toque, the green crepe trimmed with tiny white roses, a last adjustment and was just reaching for her gloves when a knock sounded at the door of her bedchamber.

"Her ladyship's compliments, miss, and she would like to see you in the library," said the young footman when Dorinda opened the door.

"Thank you, Wilcox," said Dorinda composedly. After the footman had left, she pulled on her elbow-length gloves with steady fingers, picked up her reticule, and walked to the door, pausing on the threshold to glance over the pretty, comfortable room. Despite her calm outward appearance, she could feel the muscles of her stomach contracting painfully, and she wondered if she would still be occupying her bedchamber after this evening. It was now a week since her angry exchange with Shalford in Hyde Park, and daily, hourly, she had been expecting this summons from her employer. She had little doubt that the duke had just requested Lady Torrington to dismiss her and that the dowager would comply with the request as a matter of course.

Dorinda lingered at the door of the bedchamber. If she had only held her tongue with Shalford, if she had been a trifle more meek . . . But no. She compressed her lips defiantly. She could not bring herself to regret having stood her ground with this unfair, domineering man. She was only sorry that her mother would suffer from her behavior.

When Dorinda entered the library, Lady Torrington was seated at a desk, dealing herself a game of Patience. Like Dorinda, she was dressed for an evening engagement, in a handsome gown of dark blue sarsenet. As Dorinda glanced at the slender ivory and gold cane that was propped against the side of the dowager's chair, she reflected wryly that Lady Torrington's famous gout was largely a figment of the imagination, to be trotted out when it suited her purpose. Dorinda had long since decided that it was not the dowager's health that prevented her from chaperoning Letty through the many engagements of the London season but a simple lack of inclination. The truth was that Lady Torrington had her own active social life. Her large circle of elderly cronies shared her passion for cards, and hardly a night went by that she did not sit down at one of their tables for a profitable—for she was a lucky gambler and rarely lost—high-stake game of picquet.

She raised her head now to direct a long considering stare at Dorinda. "I don't recall seeing that before," she said. "That" was a pale green crepe dress with short, full puff sleeves of intermixed green and white crepe and a skirt finished with a rouleau of white crepe intertwined with seed pearls. Completing the costume was a China crepe scarf in pale green embroidered with white flowers. "I was of two minds about allowing you to choose your own wardrobe," the dowager continued, "but I soon realized that I was right to give you your head. You have excellent taste, Miss Hayle. It's rather a pity, really, that you aren't a younger woman with a respectable, if small, dowry. You would probably find it quite easy to catch a suitable husband. Although there would always be the problem of your birth, of course."

Dorinda found it easier than usual to tamp down her resentment at Lady Torrington's casual, and oft-repeated, assumption that she was an overaged spinster with a questionable background, even though she was honest enough to admit that the dowager's opinion would probably be echoed by most of the older woman's friends if they knew Dorinda's story. No, what caught Dorinda's attention now was the dowager's relatively complaisant manner. Was it possible that Shalford had not complained to her after all? Because, surely, if Lady Torrington had summoned her granddaughter's companion to the library to dismiss her, she would not now be throwing compliments Dorinda's way?

But Dorinda's relief was short-lived for Lady Torrington said, "Well, sit down, Miss Hayle. We must have a little talk." However, the dowager merely went on to say with a wintry smile, "I thought it only proper to tell you that I am pleased, on the whole, with the way you have carried out your duties thus far. Letty has been successfully launched in London society, and you've managed to keep her out of any outrageous scrapes. I suspect that it hasn't been easy. Letty's been high-spirited and mischievous from her cradle."

Gratified, Dorinda tried not to let her pleasure show as she replied, "High-spirited, yes, but I don't agree that she is mischievous. Letty doesn't have an unkind bone in her body. I've grown very fond of her."

"And she of you, I think." Lady Torrington paused thoughtfully. "I hear from all sides that Letty is well on her way to becoming the reigning belle of the season. Only the other day, her godmother, Lady Lynnfield, told me that

Lord Bellcaster, who must have eighty thousand a year if he has a penny, seems seriously smitten. It would be a good match, of course, if . . . But no matter. I've already refused several offers for Letty's hand that were very nearly as good."

"Lord Bellcaster." Dorinda wrinkled her brow, finding it somewhat difficult to recall the tall, rather personable young man, who was only one of Letty's large retinue of admirers. "I don't think that Letty is particularly impressed with Lord Bellcaster. Though that's not surprising, since—"

"Since she's secretly betrothed to the Duke of Shalford," finished Lady Torrington dryly. "Exactly. But what I *do* find surprising is the complete lack of rumor from the gossip mills that my granddaughter is being courted by the most eligible man in England. Don't you find that strange, Miss Hayle?"

Dorinda looked at Lady Torrington with dawning comprehension. So this was the reason for her summons to the library, not merely a desire on the dowager's part to utter a gracious "Well done."

"I'm not sure that I understand," Dorinda temporized, though she had a fair idea of what Lady Torrington meant. "Are you saying? . . ."

"I'm saying that if, at any time during well-nigh the past twenty years, the Duke of Shalford had expressed even a mild interest in a young woman, society would have had him married off to her before he could blink an eye. But he never did express such an interest—well, not in a respectable woman, at any rate. Heaven knows that he's had a perfect harem of fancy pieces in his keeping, but that's neither here nor there. It was understood that Shalford wasn't the marrying kind, that he had a ready-made heir in his nephew and didn't need to consider the succession. Well, now he does wish to marry, and he has told me that he is very much in love with my granddaughter. That being the case, why isn't all London aware that he's courting Letty? What I want to know from you, Miss Hayle, is this: Has Shalford tired of Letty? Or is she discouraging him because she has met another man that she prefers to him?"

"As far as I'm aware, the duke cares deeply for Letty, and she has not met anybody that she prefers to him," replied Dorinda firmly. "Of course, he's very discreet in his attentions to her, and, as you know she is always surrounded by a swarm of young men. In my opinion, the public has simply failed to notice that the duke has entered a very crowded field! In fact, it's my guess that he has gone out of his way to hide his interest in Letty. I recall your telling me several months ago that he had insisted on postponing the announcement of their betrothal until the autumn, so that Letty could enjoy the season unhampered by any prior commitments."

"That's true. I certainly would have thought, however, that *some* whisper of gossip would have surfaced by this time. But there, if Shalford wishes to conduct his courtship discreetly—one is tempted to call it *invisibly!*—that is his affair. Well, I thank you, Miss Hayle, for this reassurance. I won't keep you. Where are you and Letty off to this evening?"

"To Almack's."

"Ah, the Wednesday night ritual! One of the pleasures of growing old, my dear, is that one is no longer obliged to accompany one's young relatives to Almack's," said the dowager frankly. "It's quite the dullest place in town. But I'm sure that Letty and her girlish friends will enjoy it exceedingly."

Lady Torrington was undoubtedly right about Almack's, thought Dorinda as she gazed up at the musicians' gallery where the orchestra was desultorily tuning up. Now that she thought about it, it was difficult to understand why admis-

sion to these three rooms in King Street, where a ball and a
supper were given every Wednesday night by subscription
during the season, was so ardently sought after. The dancing
was decorous in the extreme, under the watchful eyes of the
seven official chaperons, and the refreshment consisted of
little more than lemonade and tea, bread and butter, and
cake. Yet for all but the favored few like Letty, who took her
attendance as a matter of course, a voucher to Almack's
represented the pinnacle of social success.

From Lady Torrington and her opinions, Dorinda's
thoughts wandered inevitably to Shalford. Her brows knit as
she wondered again why the duke had not carried out his
implied threat to have her dismissed from the dowager's
employ. Perhaps he still intended to do so, but, like a cat
with a mouse, was allowing her to stew in her own anxiety
before snapping shut the trap? Only a few moments ago,
however, he had greeted her pleasantly before whisking
Letty away to enjoy a glass of lemonade.

"La, sir, you're trying to turn me up sweet. I'm very far
from being the most beautiful girl in the room tonight."

Dorinda was seated with Lady Lionel and her daughter,
and now she looked up to see Emily Leyburne blushing
furiously under the practiced gallantry of Sir Fabian
Mordaunt. But Emily is not actually embarrassed, thought
Dorinda with some surprise, only shy; Emily did not really
dislike Sir Fabian's compliments. For the first time, gazing
at the equerry's fair curls, aquiline features, and brilliant
smile, Dorinda had to admit the possibility that some
women might find the man attractive. He had as usual
scarcely glanced at Dorinda.

"No, no. I won't admit to an error in judgment," insisted
Sir Fabian. "You are indeed the most beautiful girl present
tonight, Miss Leyburne, but *not* the most beautiful *woman*.
That honor belongs to your mama."

After Emily, laughing prettily, had gone off on Sir

Fabian's arm to join a quadrille that was then forming, Dorinda said tentatively to Lady Lionel, whose lips were curved in a pleased little smile, "Emily and Sir Fabian seem to be very good friends."

"Why, yes, I hope so—" Lady Lionel interrupted herself, her cheeks turning faintly pink. "I didn't mean—that is to say, Sir Fabian is not *courting* Emily. He's only being charming to her because of his . . . well, his old friendship with me." She lowered her voice. "Even if he were interested in Emily in *that* way, you understand, it wouldn't be of the slightest use. Neither of them has enough money to live on. No, Fabian has set his cap for another lady entirely. There she is, in the quadrille just in front of us. The girl in pink sarsenet with the diamonds in her hair."

The girl in question, though woman might be a more accurate descriptive, since she was certainly older than Dorinda, was short and dumpy and plain of face. Her gown was overly fussy and unsuitable to her figure and coloring.

"She looks familiar," said Dorinda. "I believe that she was pointed out to me the other evening at Lady Lynnfield's. Isn't she the new heiress?"

"Indeed she is. That's Adelaide Ware . . . or, more properly, the Baroness Caldecott. She must be pinching herself at odd moments, when she stops to consider what a difference a few short months have made in her life. Just imagine, my dear, until very recently Adelaide was a nobody, living with her widowed mother, the wife of a recently deceased squire, in the wilds of Lincolnshire. Adelaide and her mother were living in near penury. Then suddenly the girl discovered that she had inherited the fortune *and* the title of Hector Mossley, the last Baron Caldecott. It was such a distant kinship that she was actually unaware that she was related to the baron. And until a search was made, it was assumed that Lord Caldecott had no living heirs, that the title would lapse."

"But why didn't the title lapse?" asked a puzzled Dorinda. "Miss Ware's surname wasn't Mossley, so she couldn't have descended through the male line, and as a female I don't see how she could succeed to the title in her own right. Unless it's a Scottish title. I understand that a few Scottish peerages can be inherited by women."

"Oh, no, my dear. The Barony of Caldecott is definitely an English peerage, one of the very oldest ones. It has something to do with the way the barony was created, by writ rather than by Letters Patent. But it's not a matter that I understand at all. If you'd like to know more about it, you must ask Justin."

Thinking with a twinge of distaste that even so unattractive a girl as Adelaide Ware deserved better of matrimony than the fortune-hunting Sir Fabian, Dorinda was about to disclaim any intention of applying to Shalford for information when her attention was caught by a slight commotion at the entrance to the ballroom. The man standing there, seemingly oblivious to the curious looks he was receiving, was exceptionally handsome, with a pale face and a wealth of chestnut curls. He wore an unconventional open shirt with a formal black coat and knee breeches, and his graceful stance disguised the fact that he had a deformed foot.

"My word, I never thought to see Lord Byron at Almack's," murmured Lady Lionel.

"Nor I. I should think it would be much too tame for him!" Dorinda scanned the crowd around Byron. "I don't see Lady Caroline Lamb. Perhaps she's waiting for Lord Byron outside Almack's, disguised as a pageboy. I hear that she enjoys pranks like that. I wonder if it could possibly be true, the story I heard the other day about Lady Caroline?"

"The one where she was brought to the dinner table, completely naked, in a covered silver dish?" Lady Lionel paused, her face turning a fiery red.

Dorinda began to laugh. "Now that I think of it, it does

sound very unappetizing." After a moment, a startled Lady Lionel joined her in helpless laughter.

"By Jove, if the joke is that good, you must share it with me."

"Good evening, Mr. Lacey. Actually, the joke wasn't a very good one. I don't think that you would be interested." Lady Lionel hastily changed the subject. "You're breathing hard. Have you been running?"

Perry mopped his brow. "Haven't I, though! I was afraid that I wouldn't get to Almack's in time to be admitted. You know that they close the doors here at eleven. If I were the Prince Regent himself, I wouldn't be allowed to enter a minute after the hour. Do you think I might have a dance with Miss Leyburne?" he added hopefully.

"I'm fairly sure that all of Emily's dances are spoken for," Lady Lionel said gently. "She's a very popular girl, Mr. Lacey."

"Lord, don't I know that," muttered Perry, his mobile face turning downcast.

Dorinda, who by now was on very good terms with the boy, tried to cheer him up. "Letty and I did so enjoy your parade at the Horse Guards last Sunday."

"It did go well, didn't it?" replied Perry, brightening. "But of course parading is one thing, action quite another," he added discontentedly. "How I wish that they would send us to the Peninsula. I just heard that Wellington's army is concentrated on the Agueda, and he'll be advancing against old Marmont and the Army of Portugal very soon now."

"Perhaps the army will send the Household Brigade to the Peninsula next year," Dorinda said by way of comfort, though privately she found it hard to understand the male urge to shed blood.

The quadrille having ended, the duke was coming off the floor with Letty just as Sir Fabian brought Emily to her mother's side. The two men greeted each other coolly,

Shalford giving Sir Fabian the barest nod, the baronet bowing curtly and moving off immediately. This was the first occasion during which Dorinda had seen the two together since their confrontation at the theatre in Brighton. It is obvious, she thought with a little quiver of apprehension, that their relationship has mended only to the mere brink of civility.

Soon Dorinda was trying to follow several parallel conversations. She chatted with Lady Lionel while Perry was trying to coax Emily to give him a dance already promised to someone else and Letty was deeply absorbed in talk with Shalford.

"Perry, guess what," Letty raised her voice excitedly. "The duke has just bought a new colt, by Waxey out of Penelope, a grandson of Eclipse."

"Well, if that don't beat the deuce," beamed Perry, his interest in dancing vanishing. "What's his name, sir?"

"I haven't decided." Shalford turned to Letty with a smile. "Perhaps you could suggest a name, Lady Letitia."

Letty looked pleased. "Let me think. What color is he?"

"Sorrel colored."

"What about naming him after the Golden...the Golden something—*you* know, Perry, that story about the old Greek who was always sailing away to search for the Golden...the Golden—"

"Lord, Letty, surely you don't expect me to remember anything about those old Greeks," expostulated Perry. "Even when I was at Eton I couldn't tell one of 'em from the other."

"Do you mean Jason and the Golden Fleece?" asked Shalford, a tremor of amusement in his voice.

Letty's furrowed brow cleared. "That's it. Why don't you call your new colt the 'Golden Fleece'?"

"That's a capital name, sir," said Perry enthusiastically.

"You're going to race him, surely? With a pedigree like the Fleece's, he'll be a champion in his first season."

Emily's partner for the next dance arrived just then, and Perry, gazing wistfully after the pair, said to Letty, "At least you're going to give me a dance, aren't you?"

"Well, of course, Perry. I wouldn't care for you to be a wallflower. Besides, you told me that you were coming tonight, and I saved a dance for you."

As they went off, Perry mentioned a letter from home informing him that his favorite bitch had just given birth to fourteen pups. Responding instantly, Letty exclaimed, "One of them is mine. Recall, you promised me a pup out of the last litter, and then you forgot and gave them all away."

"They're very good friends, aren't they?" murmured Shalford, as he watched Letty and Perry take their places for the country dance.

To which Dorinda, moved by some odd quality in Shalford's voice and forgetting momentarily the strain of their last meeting, replied quickly, "Oh, yes, they've been friends since they were babies. They were practically reared together."

"Yes, they seem almost like brother and sister," smiled Lady Lionel. "They remind me of the way Emily and Edmund—" She stopped suddenly, biting her lip, then hastily changed the subject. "Justin, Miss Hayle was just asking me about titles descending through the female line. I told her that you would know all about it."

As Shalford turned his full attention on Dorinda, his eyes narrowed in an expression with which she had grown familiar in the past weeks, as if, just for a moment, he had placed a vagrant memory. In an effort to distract his thoughts, she said quickly, "I know, of course, that Scottish titles can go in the female line—"

"Not all Scottish titles," he corrected her. "Only some earldoms and lordships. In England, the only peerages that can descend through females are those baronies—and there are very few of them—whose creations were authorized originally by a royal writ rather than by Letters Patent. In other words, the ancestor of such a peer must have been summoned in the very early days by an individual royal writ to a full Parliament. As such, the title can pass through either males or females, the heirs general rather than the heirs male. I suppose you're thinking of Mordaunt," he added with a curl of his lip, as he watched Sir Fabian go down the line with the dumpy new heiress, Adelaide Ware. "It's rather a sudden interest on Mordaunt's part, wouldn't you say? But then, as I understand it, he's outrun the constable."

Lady Lionel said suddenly, "Will you excuse me, Miss Hayle, Justin? I must speak to Lady Jersey for a moment."

After she had left, Shalford said regretfully, "I shouldn't have said that. Mordaunt's a gazetted fortune-hunter, and I can't stand the sight of him, but Julia has a certain soft spot in her heart for him. You may have heard that at one time, when they were very young, they wanted to marry."

Dorinda looked away, embarrassed at the frankness of his admission. "I must ask you to excuse me too, Your Grace," she said stiffly. "I see Lady Lynnfield over there—"

"Please don't go, Miss Hayle," Shalford said quietly, placing his hand on her arm to prevent her from rising. When she looked down at her arm in flustered surprise, he removed his hand, saying, "I must have a word with you."

Dorinda sat still, waiting for the axe to fall. Either Shalford had remembered their encounter in Brighton, or he was about to tell her just what punishment he proposed to mete out to her for her rudeness to him in Hyde Park. An instinct for survival prompted her to attempt to mollify Shalford, but to her horror she found herself saying belligerently, "I hope that you don't expect me to apologize for what I said to you the other day, sir. You were entirely in the wrong."

"I quite agree with you. I was about to apologize to *you*," replied Shalford dryly.

"Oh . . ." Dorinda felt her mouth gaping in chagrin. "That's . . . that's not at all necessary, Your Grace. Perhaps I said—as a matter of fact, I *did* say—some rather unfortunate things myself."

"Well, you certainly didn't mince your words," Shalford rejoined calmly. "But be that as it may, Miss Hayle, you must allow me to apologize. I don't do it very often, and I'm sure that it must be good for my soul."

Suddenly he smiled. It was a smile of such warmth, such radiance, that it transformed his aloof, slightly world-weary face. Dorinda's heart gave a lurch. For the first time, she was viewing him, not as a sexual predator, not as a potential denouncer, not even as Letty's future husband, but simply as an unusually attractive, vibrantly magnetic man whose narrowed dark gaze was arousing in her unfamiliar feelings of sensual awareness.

"I fear that my conduct was out of line from beginning to end," Shalford continued. "First off, I shouldn't have rebuked you for allowing Lady Letty to ride in young Lacey's phaeton. He's an old family friend, and it was unexceptionable of him to invite her to drive with him in a public place. Nor can I really fault *him* for letting Letty take the reins. I have an idea that she can twist him around her little finger and always has done so!" He began to laugh. "What's more, Lacey is fully aware that she's a superb driver. She was handling the ribbons of his pair like a nonesuch among the whips. But of course, it won't do. A high-perch phaeton is simply not a lady's carriage." Shalford's face darkened. "It's not a safe carriage for any-one for that matter. My heart was in my mouth when I saw Letty taking that bend at such speed. For a moment, I could actually see her lying in the roadway, her limbs at an unnatural angle, her head covered with blood. . . ."

Clenching his jaw, Shalford looked away for a moment. "Forgive me, Miss Hayle. I don't mean to enact a Cheltenham tragedy. Perhaps you haven't heard that I lost my nephew and heir in a carriage accident only a few months ago."

"Yes, I had heard. I'm sorry."

"Thank you. No point in dwelling on it, of course." He lifted his shoulders as if to exorcise a ghost. "Well, to get on with it, quite aside from the fact that I have no official standing as her fiance," he went on, "I really can't find it in my heart to blame Letty herself for this escapade. She's naturally impulsive and high-spirited, and she must have been chafing at her lack of opportunity to ride since her arrival in London. She *should* ride, and so should you as her chaperon. So I've ordered sent up, from my estate in Oxfordshire, a gentle young mare for your use. My own groom will come over to Torrington House every day to give you riding lessons. Soon you'll be able to accompany Lady Letitia on her rides, and we'll all be happier."

If asked, Dorinda would have found it difficult to state which of her mixed bag of feelings was uppermost in her consciousness. She was relieved that she had been dissolved of blame for Letty's brush with danger in Perry's phaeton. She was mildly flattered that Shalford had sent all the way to Oxfordshire for a mount for her use and that he had appointed his own groom to give her riding lessons, but at the same time she felt resentful that, in his usual domineering style, he had not bothered to ask her preferences in the matter. And last of all, lurking in the back of her mind, was a thought that she hesitated to articulate; she had a feeling of vague dissatisfaction, almost of regret, that all Shalford's efforts were aimed at maintaining Letty's contentment and ease of mind, which he obviously equated with his own

Quite naturally so, Dorinda told herself, so why should she feel this illogical sense of disappointment?

"Well, Miss Hayle?"

"Thank you very much, Your Grace. I think it would be an excellent idea if I learned to ride."

Seemingly satisfied with Dorinda's rather colorless reply, Shalford rose, extending his hand. "Famous! That's settled then. And now, since a new quadrille is forming, would you care to dance, Miss Hayle? Lady Letitia has informed me that all the rest of her dances are taken, so unless you take pity on me I shall be quite out in the cold!"

Sternly suppressing a pang of resentment that she had been asked to partner Shalford only because Letty was engaged elsewhere, Dorinda took his arm and moved with him to the dance floor. As she felt the sinewy strength of the arm beneath the fine black broadcloth, her thoughts unwillingly reverted to that evening in the Green Room at Brighton, when for a few brief moments she had longed to be clasped even closer in this man's hard embrace.

Chapter VII

Before leaving the room, Dorinda stole another look at herself in her new riding habit, the first that she had ever owned, a well-tailored creation in pale blue broadcloth piped in black, worn with a dashing Hussar's bonnet trimmed with waving plumes. As she started down the stairs she thought with satisfaction that these early morning riding lessons were going very well, that in a few days she would be accomplished enough to go riding with Letty in Hyde Park.

The sound of rattling dishes caught her attention, and she paused, turning her head to glance back down the corridor, where she spotted Betsy Morris, Letty's abigail, coming out of Letty's bedchamber with a laden tray.

"Good morning, Betsy. Lady Letitia must have awakened very early this morning."

A startled, faintly guilty look crossed the abigail's face. "Oh, yes, ma'am. Her ladyship woke up *very* early. Matter of fact, she just couldn't seem to get to sleep at all last night."

Dorinda was immediately suspicious. She had never known Letty to suffer from a moment's insomnia. Moreover, the girl, like Lady Torrington, usually slept late, rarely emerging from her bedchamber until midmorning.

"Well, Betsy, since Lady Letitia is already awake, I think that I will just have a word with her before I go out riding."

"Oh, no, ma'am. I shouldn't do that if I was you. Her ladyship said . . . she said that she was beginning to feel sleepy at last after drinking her tea and she might go back to bed for a little nap," floundered Betsy, never quick-witted at the best of times.

"I don't think Lady Letitia will object to my coming in," said Dorinda pleasantly. "You can go along to the kitchen, Betsy."

Knocking perfunctorily, Dorinda entered Letty's bed-chamber to find the girl fully dressed in a sprigged muslin morning gown. A long gray cloak, which Dorinda thought she recognized, was draped carelessly over a chair.

"Dorinda! What are you? . . . Did you want something?" Letty was doing her best to seem composed, but her mobile face displayed even more confusion than had Betsy's.

Dorinda raised an eyebrow. "Well, Letty? Have you been strolling along St. James Street again?" she asked, glancing significantly at the gray cloak.

"I . . . yes. I know that you don't like the idea of it, Dorinda, but I see no harm in it," replied Letty defensively.

"At this hour? Come now, you know as well as I do that the dandies don't go to their clubs until midafternoon. Where did you really go this morning?"

Cornered, Letty replied sulkily, "If you must have it, I walked with Betsy down Berkeley Street to Piccadilly, where Mr. Barry picked us up in a hack and we drove to the Green Park. Then Mr. Barry and I strolled about for a bit. But you needn't worry that I scandalized anybody, or anything of that sort. There was nobody else around so early in the day—nobody who mattered, anyway—and besides, who would recognize me in Cook's old cloak?"

Dorinda gasped in surprise. "You went to the Green Park with Desmond? What on earth possessed you to do such a thing? And I don't understand . . . how did Desmond arrange such a meeting?"

"Oh, he sent me a note a week or so ago. I've met him several times since then. He wanted to talk about you."

"Me!"

"Yes. You hurt his feelings very much that day in Hyde Park when you told him that you couldn't be friends with him anymore. He thought, if he talked to me, that I might suggest some way of bringing you two back together again. Dorinda, how could you be so cruel to Mr. Barry? An old friend like that!"

"Letty, we've talked about this previously. You must know that your grandmother would object very much to my open friendship with an actor. Recall, I've even had to hide the fact that my own mother once belonged to the profession! It may seem unfair, but stage folk are just not considered respectable."

As Dorinda spoke, she began to sense that the situation was not as straightforward as it appeared. Did Desmond really think that Letty's intervention would heal his breach with Dorinda? Or did he have some other purpose in mind? He was an actor to his fingertips, and it was sometimes difficult to know when he was merely playing a part. She asked Letty skeptically, "If your object in meeting Desmond was to reconcile the two of us, why is it that you haven't so much as mentioned his name to me?" Another thought struck her. "Letty! You don't—You can't fancy yourself in love with Desmond?"

"Of course not," exclaimed Letty indignantly. "You know very well that my . . . my affections are already engaged.

And besides, Mr. Barry is practically an old man. He must be well over thirty!"

Younger than Shalford, thought Dorinda, and mentally chastised herself as Letty went on talking.

"It's just that it's so good to *talk* to Mr. Barry," Letty said wistfully. "He's lived such an interesting life, he's always been able to do just as he likes. And my life here in London . . . it's so dull, always the same, day after day. We pay our morning calls, and once a week we go to Almack's, and every night there's some kind of party, or ball, or rout. All very much alike, even to seeing the same people at each event. Last night at Lady Armistead's house there must have been near a thousand guests in rooms that shouldn't have held half that many. We had to fight our way up the stairs, and then there was no music, no cards, not even any conversation. We just elbowed our way from room to room and then clawed our way back down the stairs to wait in line for what seemed like hours for our carriage. Why, Godmama fainted in the crush!"

"Yes, poor Lady Lynnfield. We must send around today to inquire about her health. Well, I agree, Letty, that last night was the outside of enough. But you shouldn't refine too much on it. Not all our engagements are dead bores, certainly. And you must remember, after you're married you'll be expected to preside over many such affairs. It's good training for you."

A little cloud descended over Letty's face. "Yes, I know. Grandmama says that in a few years I'll probably be *the* society hostess. Lady Melbourne, Lady Holland, people like that—they're all getting older, and Grandmama says that someone must eventually take their places as leaders of society. But not just yet, Dorinda, not while I'm still so young."

Dorinda eyed Letty sympathetically. She had been thinking for some time that, however fond Letty was of Shalford, the girl was not really ready to assume so illustrious a place in society. She needed another season, another year, in which to grow and mature. However, there was nothing Dorinda could do about the marriage plans. She must just see to what Lady Torrington had hired her to do, guard the restless Letty and keep her from plunging into a situation that might cause a huge scandal.

"I'm sorry, Letty," Dorinda said now. "I like Desmond very much, and I know what good company he can be. But you must see that these meetings with him just won't do. Selfishly, I must point out that if your grandmother discovered I was allowing you to see Desmond, she would discharge me immediately."

Letty sighed. "Yes, I know. Grandmama would have a fit of the vapors if she found out about Mr. Barry." A flash of her usual buoyancy lit up her eyes, and she giggled, saying, "It was no great thing anyway, you know, getting up at the crack of dawn to stroll in the Green Park. I was quite ready to come home because my slippers were completely soaked from the wet grass."

Belatedly, Dorinda went down to the stables, where she found Shalford's diffident young groom waiting patiently for her. Today, however, though the morning was bright and beautiful, and the groom shyly told her that she was doing "werry well, miss," Dorinda derived little pleasure from her ride. Her thoughts were concentrated on Letty's latest escapade, and knowing Desmond's powers of persuasion, Dorinda was not at all sure that her charge would resist another overture from that practiced charmer.

Later that afternoon Dorinda came to a conclusion. Pleading a headache, she cut short the daily drive in Hyde Park. After she and Letty had returned to Torrington House, Dorinda went to the wardrobe in her bedchamber where, behind all her fine new dresses, she reached for the plain black dress and the modest black pelisse and bonnet that she had worn while she was in mourning for her stepfather. Quickly changing clothes, Dorinda left the house by a back entrance and walked to Piccadilly Street, where she hailed a hackney cab to take her to Covent Garden. First, however, she had the driver take her to St. Martin's Lane just off Leicester Square. There, she entered a milliner's shop that she and Letty had previously noted but had never visited.

"A black veil, madame? Why, certainly. A sudden bereavement, perhaps?" said the sympathetic proprietress.

"Yes, very sudden. It's my poor husband . . . he died suddenly last night," declared Dorinda, lying boldly and wiping away an imaginary tear. As she looked at her reflection in the mirror, adjusting the voluminous veil over her bonnet, she thought with satisfaction that there was little chance she would be recognized if she happened to meet any of her recent London acquaintances.

Arriving at the theatre in Covent Garden, Dorinda entered the lobby rather nervously. It still lacked almost an hour to the evening performance, but there were already several young dandies in the lobby. Boisterous and half-inebriated, they ogled and flirted with a group of flashily dressed young girls in the tow of several older women in shapeless, long black cloaks. The emptiness in the girls' faces, and the venal calculation in those of the older women, repelled Dorinda, and she timidly inquired of the ticket seller the location of the stage entrance. From there she found her way to the Green Room. She paused nervously just inside the door, asking a passing actor who stared curiously at her deep mourning, to notify Desmond that a friend wished to see him. As she sat down in an inconspicuous chair in a corner of the room she noted vaguely that many of the players were already present, chatting with each other or with visitors, checking their stage costumes or makeup in the large mirror over the mantel or in a movable swing glass.

Hearing a loud, familiar giggle, Dorinda looked up, only to be frozen into shocked immobility when she spotted Cassandra Bell standing very close to Shalford and gazing laughingly up into his face.

Dorinda had never especially cared for the principal actress of Desmond's provincial touring company. Cassandra was coarse and pushy, despite her undeniable talent and good looks, and her jealousy had erupted in almost daily emotional tempests during the brief period in Brighton when Dorinda had usurped her leading place in the company. Tonight Cassandra was apparently captivating Shalford who, it seemed to Dorinda's bemused gaze, had cast off his normal personality like the moulting of a dragonfly. Here was no king of the Corinthians, aloof, correct, faintly bored. Shalford's lips were wreathed in an appreciative smile and his dark eyes gleamed with a knowing laughter. As Dorinda watched, he placed a caressing finger under Cassandra's chin and leaned down to whisper something in her ear that caused her to bridle coquettishly. Just like . . . Dorinda found her fingers digging convulsively into the material of her skirt as she tried to evade a nagging memory.

Apparently His Grace the Duke of Shalford divided all women into two categories and treated them accordingly, Dorinda thought scornfully: females of his own class, whom he placed on a pedestal and to whom he reacted with a kind of bloodless, languid civility; and women of the lower orders, with whom he was able to shed the inhibitions of background and breeding.

"Good evening, ma'am. You wanted to see me?" Desmond, dressed for his part in *Coriolanus* in a breastplate and plumed helmet, stood in front of her, his eyebrows raised inquiringly.

"It's I, Desmond. Please sit down. I must talk to you."

"Dorinda! What are you? . . ."

"Please, Desmond, keep your voice down. I don't want anyone to recognize me."

Sitting down beside her, Desmond stared at her black dress and heavy mourning veil. "Lord, I'd defy anybody to recognize you looking like that. There's nobody here anyway who . . . oh." His eyes followed hers as she glanced at Cassandra and Shalford. "You do know that swell, don't you? I'm told he's a regular visitor to the Green Room. In fact, last season he was very smitten with Cynthia Cox; she played Emilia in that performance of *Othello* that you attended a few weeks ago. Come to think of it, I haven't noticed him much in evidence since I rejoined the company. By Jove, though, I can understand why you wouldn't want Shalford to know that you were visiting me. The rumor is that he has a case on your little charge, Lady Letitia. Is that true?"

"I couldn't say," replied Dorinda guardedly. "Desmond, why are you meeting secretly with Letty?"

"Oh, ho. So you've heard about my trysts with the fair Letty." Desmond grinned. "I didn't think that it would take you very long to find out about them."

"What do you mean? You wanted me to find out that you were meeting Letty?"

"Yes, I did." Desmond shrugged. "It seemed like an excellent idea at the time, but . . . What the deuce, Dorinda, I was so angry with you for pushing me out of your life, I decided to pay you back in your own coin by making friends with Lady Letty. I knew that would get a rise out of you. And then, you know, after a bit, I quite enjoyed our walks in the park. She's a taking little thing, is Letty."

"A rise? Desmond, are you mad? Don't you realize that this is the kind of thing that could ruin Letty's reputation, make it impossible for her to make a good marriage?"

"I must say, I don't much like your implication that I'm some kind of moral leper. Associating with me isn't going to send that chit down the road to perdition," rejoined Desmond, his face darkening.

Dorinda threw up her hands. "I didn't mean anything of the sort. There's nothing that I would like better than to have you as my friend here in London. I wish that you could be Letty's friend too, because she enjoys your company, and she certainly likes you better than most of the young fops that she's been meeting. But we can't change the rules of society. If it ever became known that Letty was having clandestine meetings with an actor, her fiancé would cry off immediately from their engagement." Dorinda stopped in consternation.

"An engagement, is it?" Desmond whistled silently. "That sly puss! She never said a word to me about it, and believe me, she talks more than any female I have ever met."

"It's . . . it's a secret engagement. I shouldn't have told you about it. Desmond, promise me that you won't mention it to anyone."

"Mum's the word, now that you've asked me so prettily. But just between the two of us, who's the lucky man? It's not? . . . Dorinda! You don't need to tell me. Our Letty is going to be the next Duchess of Shalford!"

As another shout of laughter came from Cassandra Bell, the harassed Dorinda tossed her head under the sheltering veil, muttering petulantly, "Don't be so sure about that, Desmond Barry. His High and Mightiness seems to have found other interests."

"You mean the duke and Cassy?" asked Desmond in surprise. "What a green girl you are still, Dorinda. All these fancy fellows on the town have their bits of muslin on the side, but it don't mean anything. Cassy certainly knows that the duke is just having a bit of fun."

"Good. I'm glad to know that Cassandra is in no danger of having her heart broken," said Dorinda coldly. "What *does* concern me, however, is Letty's welfare. Desmond, I'd like your promise that you won't invite her for any more early morning walks in the park."

"My heart's delight, you know that I can't refuse you anything," declaimed Desmond dramatically. Reverting to his usual tones, he said with a grin, "Actually, I was getting a bit tired of those meetings. Most actors hate getting up early in the morning, and I'm no exception. And, to be honest, I was also becoming a bit tired of Letty. I'm attracted to more mature women, women with a little spice in their characters, someone more like you."

"Desmond, we've been all over this before and—"

"Rest easy, my sweet. I'm now ready to admit that I've no place in Letty's world—or in yours, at least for the time being. You have my promise: Lady Letitia is safe from the likes of me."

"Thank you, Desmond. I *knew* that I could count on you," said Dorinda fervently.

"That's not to say that I've given up my designs on *you,* however," Desmond resumed. "Am I right in assuming that we can be friends again when you are no longer in Lady Torrington's employ?"

"I . . . yes. Of course."

"So when will that be? The old lady engaged you to chaperone Lady Letty just for the season, I believe. Or will you be staying on to help with the preparations for the ducal wedding?"

Dorinda caught her breath as she realized that for many weeks she had not been giving any thought to what she would be doing after the month of July. It had been understood, at the time the dowager had engaged her to be Letty's companion, that she would be returning to Eastfield and her mother's house at the end of the season. So why, now, did the thought of leaving London suddenly fill her with such a sense of emptiness, of desolation? She answered Desmond calmly, however, saying, "No, I won't have anything to do with the preparations for Letty's wedding. I'll be going back to Eastfield at the end of July."

"Splendid. The Theatre Royal will close for the rest of the summer about then. I'll come down to see you and Lady Roger." A callboy poked his head inside the door of the Green Room to make his first shrill call, and Desmond rose, saying regretfully, "I'd best be going. Good-bye, Dorinda. Expect me in Eastfield the day after we ring down the curtain for our final performance of the season."

"Good-bye, Desmond, I look forward to seeing you."

Outside the Doric portico of the theatre, Dorinda made her way through the throng of last-minute patrons who were hurrying to take their seats before curtain time. As she lifted her hand to catch the eye of a passing hackney cab driver, a pair of dandies, arm in arm and roisterously intoxicated, caromed into her and sent her sprawling against a tall figure behind her. A strong slender hand grasped her arm, and a familiar confident voice said, "Are you all right, ma'am? Those drunken louts didn't hurt you?"

Her heart in her mouth, Dorinda pulled away from Shalford's hand, murmuring a breathless, "Thank you, sir. I'm quite unhurt."

At the sound of her voice, Shalford started, looking at her closely through the thick mourning veil. "Have we met, ma'am?"

With the courage of despair, Dorinda decided to brazen it out. "Lor', mister, if ever I'd clapped me glaziers on a gentry cove like yerself, I'd not forget it," she chuckled coarsely, thanking her lucky stars for having listened with appreciative amusement to Peregrine Lacey's slangy prattle, generously larded with cant terms. She extended her hand to Shalford, whining, "Could ye lay out a little blunt, sir? I'm pinched for the needful, what with four babes at home and all of them mortal sick. A swell like yerself wouldn't never miss a bit o' rhino, now would ye?"

With a shrug and a cynical smile, Shalford dropped half a dozen coins into her hand. "Just don't spend it all on Blue Ruin, my girl," he advised. "Buy some food for the babies— if there are any babies. And here's something extra for a doctor in case one of those problematic babies is really sick."

Chapter VIII

The butler entered the library quietly. "Will you see His Grace the Duke of Shalford, Miss Hayle?"

Dorinda looked up in surprise, closing her book over her finger to keep her place. She was enjoying a rare afternoon of solitude, browsing in the Torrington House library, a room frequented only rarely by the dowager and practically never by the unbookish Letty. "You've informed His Grace that both Lady Torrington and Lady Letitia are out this afternoon?"

"Oh, yes, miss. His Grace has asked me to tell you that he would like a word with you, if you can spare him a few minutes."

"Certainly, Frith. Tell the duke that I will join him in the drawing room directly."

Smoothing her dress and running a nervous hand over her hair, Dorinda left the library with dragging steps and entered the drawing room. It was now over a week since her unlucky encounter with the duke at the theatre. She had seen him a number of times since then, always briefly and always in a crowd, and she was satisfied that he had not connected the beggar girl of Covent Garden with Letty's companion. But she was very unwilling to see him privately, and she was perfectly aware of the reason for her reluctance. She had been unable to crush the smoldering anger, which she freely conceded was unreasonable, that Shalford had aroused in her with his carefree pursuit of Cassandra Bell while he was demanding the utmost circumspection from his future wife.

"Good afternoon, Miss Hayle. Thank you for seeing me."

Returning Shalford's bow, Dorinda asked him to be seated, adding, "Frith tells me that you're aware that Letty has gone off shopping this afternoon with Lady Lionel and Miss Leyburne."

"So he told me. I'm not at all surprised." Shalford lifted an amused eyebrow. "Emily could talk of nothing else at breakfast except a new shop in Oxford Street that has a huge assortment of the most fetching silk ribbons imaginable, and of a tradesman who calls himself a *plumassier* and sells nothing but feathers and ostrich plumes. And so, I gather that she persuaded her mother and Lady Letitia to go shopping for these treasures before they are all snatched up by other fashionable females?"

Forcing herself to smile with him, Dorinda murmured, "Yes, it was a spur of the moment decision. They *had* been planning to visit the British Museum. I expected Letty to return by this time, but perhaps she found a great many bargains! She will be sorry to have missed you."

"It's no great matter. I shall certainly see her tonight at Lady Melbourne's," replied Shalford, shrugging his shoulders under the exquisitely cut dark blue superfine of his coat. His dark eyes fixed on her intently. "Actually, Miss Hayle, I'm rather glad to have this opportunity to speak with you alone. I've remarked often of late that you've been a most ideal companion for Lady Letitia—a true gentle-woman, modest, self-effacing, quietly instructive. Letty has blossomed into a charming, poised young woman, and I think it's about time that you received credit for helping her acquire some much-needed town bronze. Especially in view of my rude, and unjust, outburst in Hyde Park."

"Thank you, Your Grace. I've merely been carrying out my duties," replied Dorinda colorlessly, although she knew she should be registering pleasure and gratitude at his praise. But all she felt was a prickling annoyance at Shalford's unconscious condescension. However illogical the feeling, it galled her to be regarded as a "modest, self-effacing gentlewoman."

Apparently Shalford did not notice her lack of warmth. Probably he regards it as just one more instance of my self-effacing nature, Dorinda thought wryly.

"I've been casting about for some way to express my appreciation for your services," he continued, "and I do believe that I've hit on the very thing. My groom, Jarrett, tells me that you're the most apt pupil he's ever had, and I can see for myself, now that you're riding with Lady Letty in Hyde Park every day, that you're a natural horsewoman. So I've decided to present you with the horse you've been riding. As of today, Persephone is yours."

"Thank you, but no. I can't accept the horse."

The words rang out sharply, and Shalford's expectant smile faded into a puzzled frown. "May I ask why?" he inquired frigidly.

Dorinda was silent, trying to fight back the quick surge of anger that had caused her automatic rejection of his gift. Who was he, she thought hotly, to play King Cophetua to her beggar maid? Then her more rational self took over: offending the Duke of Shalford in this household might well reduce her to the status of beggar maid, or something very close to it! "It ... it's much too valuable a gift, Your

Grace," she stammered. "As I said, I was merely carrying out my duties."

His face cleared. "Please let me be the judge of that," he said indulgently. "I think you and Persephone will make a wonderful pair, and I hope you will ride her with pleasure for years to come." He reached under his striped marcella waistcoat for a heavy gold watch. "Now that we've settled that, I must be going. I look forward to seeing you and Lady Letitia at Lady Melbourne's assembly this evening."

After the duke had been shown out of the room by a solicitous Frith, Dorinda relieved her bruised feelings by hurling her light shawl to the floor and stamping on it. Feeling only marginally more cheerful, she was about to return to the library when her eye fell on the pianoforte in a corner of the drawing room. Since her arrival at Torrington House, because of the pressure of Letty's many engagements, she had had few opportunities to play the instrument, so superior to the vicar's pianoforte back in Eastfield, on which she had occasionally been invited to play after leaving Tunbridge Wells Academy. She sat down now before the instrument, playing first a snatch of Mozart and then gliding into a verse of the slow and tender Gaelic song, *"Cuir, a chinn Dìlis,"* which she had sung in Desmond's production of *The Lady of the Lake.* "O, sweetest and dearest, fairest and dearest, Take me, my darling, now in thine arms," she sang softly. Soon she was lost in the music, imagining herself back onstage as Ellen, going from the "Lament of the Border Widow" to the plaintive "The Bonny Earl of Murray."

A sound of clapping came from behind her, and she swung around to see the dowager and her ever-present elderly companion, Miss Minniott, standing near the door.

"Fanny and I heard the sound of your playing as we entered the house," said Lady Torrington, advancing into the room. "I had no idea that you were so accomplished."

"Indeed, yes. You play and sing beautifully, Miss Hayle," echoed Miss Minniott. "As well as any professional, I should say."

Lady Torrington frowned. "I don't like that word 'professional,' Fanny. Miss Hayle's mother, now—I believe *she* sang before paid audiences. But Miss Hayle is using her musical gift just as she should, as a genteel, ladylike accomplishment. Well, now, Miss Hayle, don't let us interrupt you. As a matter of fact, I should very much like to hear again that haunting little thing you were playing as we came in. Scottish, wasn't it? Do you know, Fanny, I think we might ask Miss Hayle to play for our guests some evening soon."

Ignoring the dowager's slighting reference to her mother, Dorinda turned back to the pianoforte. She was just playing the final strains of "The Bonny Earl of Murray" when the shopping party entered the drawing room.

"Oh, Miss Hayle, that was so lovely," exclaimed Emily, clapping energetically. "If I had had your talent, I shouldn't have minded taking all those singing lessons that Mama insisted upon!"

"Well, at least you can hit the right note occasionally, Emily," grinned Letty. "I sound exactly like a lovesick frog, and even Grandmama was forced to admit, finally, that I had no musical talent at all. Poor Monsieur Antoine, I think he was so relieved to be able to drop me as a pupil."

"Even if you had had a voice like Catalani, he would have been happy to be rid of you," retorted Lady Torrington. "You were fast driving the poor man to Bedlam with your pranks."

"Emily, dear, we must go home. The seamstress is coming for the final fitting of your gown," said Lady Lionel. "Lady Torrington, you *are* coming with Letty to Emily's party on Friday?"

"Why, of course. How could you think that I would miss Emily's party, Julia?" There was a faint note of reproach in the dowager's voice. It was obvious to Dorinda that Lady Torrington already considered Emily a member of the family by virtue of her uncle's marriage to Letty.

"You do recall that we're not having a ball, just a small dinner party?" asked Lady Lionel a bit anxiously. "Justin was quite put out when I wouldn't allow him to pay for a coming-out ball. But, you know, he's already been so generous to me and Emily that I just couldn't put him to any more expense."

"I'm sure that your independence does you credit, Julia." Lady Torrington smiled. But after Emily and her mother had left, the dowager remarked to Dorinda, "Julia is refining too much on her obligations to Shalford, in my opinion. He's one of the wealthiest men in England, and he can well afford any number of balls, as well as the very generous settlement that he's making on Emily."

What had been described by Lady Lionel as a small party seemed rather more than that, thought Dorinda, as she looked around the cavernous drawing room at Leyburne House, already uncomfortably crowded. Later, when she sat down to dinner in the grand ballroom, she would estimate that the long temporary tables there had been set up for more than a hundred guests.

"I'm surprised to see young Lacey here at such an intimate party," observed Lady Torrington, seated next to Dorinda, as she watched Perry making his way across the room toward them. "He's a nice boy, but there's no money at all there. Julia shouldn't encourage him to dangle after Emily." Her greeting to Perry was cordial enough, however, and she chatted with him for a few moments before moving on to speak to one of her cronies.

Perry seemed to be less than normally ebullient as he sat down to talk to Dorinda, and it developed that his thoughts were far from London, concentrated on Wellington's troops in the Peninsula. "The duke's besieging the forts in front of Salamanca and there will be a big battle there any day now," he said, sunk in gloom. "Old Marmont will soon be on the run, right out of Spain and that will be the end of my chances to get into the war before it's over."

"Oh, I don't think Napoleon will give up Spain that easily. Although, come to think of it, he may not have many extra troops to send there to reinforce Marmont, now that he's invaded Russia."

"Russia! That campaign will be over before it's started," scoffed Perry. "Boney can lick the Russkies with one hand tied behind his back." He looked across the room. "Emily— Miss Leyburne—looks charming tonight. Shall we go over and rescue her from the baroness?

"It's that tender heart of Em— of Miss Leyburne," Perry declared as he and Dorinda made their way to the other side of the room, where Emily sat talking to the new heiress, the dumpy Baroness Caldecott. "She lets that Friday-faced Lady Caldecott monopolize her company when they meet at parties. Emily says that the woman is shy and needs to make friends, but *I* say that she's an antidote and a dead bore, no matter how large her fortune is. Would you believe it, m' mother suggested that *I* offer for the baroness. Me!"

"Miss Hayle, Mr. Lacey, do sit down." Emily smiled as they approached. "Lady Caldecott has been telling me the most interesting stories about her childhood in Lincolnshire."

"Never been to Lincolnshire, but I daresay it's a capital place to live," said Perry hastily. "Miss Leyburne, you must come with me to confer with Lady Letty. She has a devilish fine scheme to organize a supper party to Vauxhall Gardens, and we must have your advice."

As Perry bore the laughing Emily away, Lady Caldecott said bruskly to Dorinda, "You needn't feel that you must stay with me, you know." Her unprepossessing face, with its small eyes and doughy features, wore an expression of supreme indifference, but as Dorinda, taken back by her near-rudeness, was about to turn away, a muscle twitched in the baroness' cheek. On an impulse, Dorinda dropped into the chair beside her. "Oh, but I should like very much to talk to you, Lady Caldecott."

The muscle twitched again. "Would you? I can't think why. That child—Emily Leyburne—always pretends to be so interested in my tiresome stories about Lincolnshire, but I know that she's just being kind." Lady Caldecott bit her lip. "I'm sorry. I don't usually say things like that."

Dorinda felt a sudden flash of enlightenment. Perry was wrong about Lady Caldecott, and Emily was right—or nearly right. The baroness was not shy, exactly, but—yes, that was the word—unsure of herself in this fashionable new world into which she had been catapulted from her nondescript life in the provinces.

"I don't think that Miss Leyburne is pretending. I've always found her to be interested in everything and everyone," Dorinda said gently. She added tentatively, "I believe that this is your first extended visit to London?"

"Yes, it is," replied the baroness shortly. "I came here once as a small child, but I don't remember anything of it."

Trying to put her companion more at ease in the conversation, Dorinda said sympathetically, "This is my first visit, too. I'd lived all my life in a tiny village near Brighton, and I felt quite overwhelmed by my first experiences of London. Sometimes I had the sensation that I had been thrown into a racing river in which I was desperately trying to find my footing so that I could wade ashore to safety."

For a few moments, as the baroness stared at her intently, Dorinda feared that her well-meant words had caused offence.

"I know why you're speaking this way, and I like you for it," said Lady Caldecott at last. "You're Lady Letitia Wingate's companion, aren't you? Some sort of poor relation? Please, I don't mean to hurt your feelings. Actually, though most people would consider my position infinitely more satisfying than yours, I rather envy you."

"You envy me?"

"Yes. You know just who you are, and exactly what your place is in society. I don't." The baroness was talking more freely now, as though she were releasing long pent-up feelings. "Like you, I grew up in a tiny village, and I never thought to leave it. There was just enough money to support my mother and me in modest comfort. I had never even heard of my father's cousin, Lord Caldecott. And then suddenly I discovered that I was his only surviving relative, that I was not only a peeress in my own right but a very wealthy one to boot. Only I didn't feel like one. I wasn't pretty, I wasn't young, I didn't know how to dress and I didn't know how to act with all the society folk whom I was meeting. I was invited everywhere, but the women either ignored me or left my company as soon as they politely could. Some of the men were quite attentive, which pleased me at first, because I would like to be married, but I soon realized that there was only one reason for their interest in me: my money."

Dorinda looked away in acute discomfort. She could think of nothing to say in the face of this shattering frankness.

The baroness laughed unexpectedly. "There, I'm glad that I've said it at last! And no, I'm not afraid that you'll tattle my remarks all over town," she added shrewdly, reading Dorinda's mind. "You're not that kind of a person. In fact, I'd like very much to be your friend."

Dorinda smiled warmly. "And I yours, Lady Caldecott."

"Won't you call me Adelaide? I can't get used to being called Lady Caldecott. She feels like a perfect stranger to me!"

"Oh, I know exactly how that is," laughed Dorinda. "I was named after a role that my mother"—she caught herself just in time—"after a role that my mother found so amusing in the play, *The Beaux' Stratagem,* but I've always had a nagging feeling that it wasn't my real name."

"Well, ladies, I'm glad to find you in such high spirits tonight."

Dorinda felt chilled as she looked up into Sir Fabian Mordaunt's smiling face. She had not expected to see him at Emily's "intimate" dinner party, although in view of the recurrent story that he and Lady Lionel had once loved each other, it was perhaps not surprising that he had been invited. Or it might even be that Lady Lionel had had a definite purpose in inviting Sir Fabian, Dorinda thought in surprise as she watched a delighted smile spread across Adelaide Caldecott's face.

"La, sir, I never thought to see you here," said the baroness archly. "I believed you to be attending the regent tonight."

"Yes, His Royal Highness was definitely promised to Lady Bessborough this evening, but unfortunately he became indisposed. Oh, nothing serious, I'm glad to say, but it does give me the opportunity to see you tonight, Lady Caldecott. May I tell you how well you look? That gown is the exact color of your eyes."

"Thank you. I was hoping that you . . . I like it very much myself. Oh, Sir Fabian, do you know Miss Hayle?"

His smile fading, Sir Fabian shifted his hooded gaze to Dorinda. "Miss Hayle?" he said vaguely. "I'm not quite sure . . ."

"Good evening, Sir Fabian. We've met before. I'm Lady Letitia Wingate's companion."

"Oh, yes, I recall now. Delighted to see you again."

Leaving Dorinda with the welcome impression that he had not really registered her presence, Sir Fabian turned his full attention back to Lady Caldecott, plying her with graceful compliments, telling her amusing anecdotes, causing her to blossom under his charm so that her plain face became almost pretty.

Dorinda sat quietly watching his performance with a growing sense of shock. With the best will in the world, she could not believe that Sir Fabian, whose amorous career was a byword and whose financial difficulties were as well known, felt any real regard for Adelaide Caldecott. A few minutes ago, the baroness had indicated a clear-minded assessment of her situation when she had told Dorinda that men were only interested in her because of her fortune. Why, then, could Adelaide not see that Sir Fabian, like all her other suitors, was pursuing her for her money? There could only be one answer to that question, Dorinda thought sadly: Adelaide's native shrewdness had dissolved away in the ecstasy of her new-found passion for the regent's equerry. Feeling both depressed and impotent, Dorinda was glad to be diverted from her concern for the baroness by the announcement that dinner was served.

Seated opposite Letty in the center of one of the long tables that had been set up in the ballroom, Dorinda stole a glance at Shalford at the head of the table. With his usual languid ease, he was chatting with Lady Torrington at his right. She thought with a flicker of amusement that he—for it must have been he—had neatly circumvented his sister-in-law's desire to make Emily's debut a modest affair. Emily's party was not the usual ball, it was true, but no expense had been spared to make the occasion one marked by the epitome of style and elegance. The tables gleamed with silver serving pieces, the walls of the room were massed with gorgeous blooms, the food included every imaginable kind of meat and game, elaborate pastries, and hothouse fruits. And Dorinda was sure that the lovely diamond bandeau in Emily's hair had been presented by Shalford to his niece.

After dinner, when the gentlemen had joined the ladies in the drawing room, the guests whiled away their time until the arrival of the tea tray with the usual post-dinner activities. Some joined the dowager in the library for one of her interminable games of picquet, others played a rubber of casino or a game of lottery tickets. Off in a corner, Sir Fabian paid devoted attendance to Adelaide Caldecott. Dorinda, for the moment alone since Letty was chatting with one of her friends, sat with her eyes fixed on the ill-sorted pair, wondering if Lady Caldecott would have even a moment of happiness if she accepted the offer that Sir Fabian was undoubtedly about to make.

"You seem very thoughtful, Miss Hayle. Are you wondering which title the baroness will use if she marries Sir Fabian? Will she elect to be called Lady Mordaunt, or will she remain Lady Caldecott?"

"No, I must confess that the question hadn't occurred to me," replied Dorinda, a little surprised that Shalford had seen fit to sit down beside her when he had a whole roomful of more important guests. For the first time, this evening, she had heard a whispered speculation or two that the duke's discreet attentions to Letty were perhaps more serious than people had supposed. Singling out Letty's companion at his niece's coming-out party could only add fuel to that speculation, Dorinda thought.

"Well, I agree, it's certainly no world-shaking problem," shrugged the duke. "One questions the baroness' good sense in marrying Mordaunt, of course, but"—he shrugged again—"it's odd how things turn out. I knew the previous Lord Caldecott quite well. He was rather a strange man, with just one overriding interest in life. He was inordinately proud of his ancestry. The peerage, you know, is one of the very oldest in the kingdom, ranking right after the Barony of de Ros, which dates back to 1264. But, oddly enough for someone so proud of his rank, Caldecott was a confirmed bachelor with no concern at all for providing for the succession. He always said vaguely that he was sure some distant cousin would carry on the title, but he made no attempt to contact his heir. I think he would have been quite surprised to discover that he would be succeeded by a woman."

"Uncle Justin, might I interrupt you for a moment? I'd like to speak to Miss Hayle."

Shalford smiled affectionately at his niece, who had come up arm in arm with Letty. "Certainly, Puss. I had no intention of monopolizing Miss Hayle."

Exchanging a mischievous glance with Letty, Emily said to Dorinda, "I have the greatest favor to ask of you."

"Why, of course. Anything at all. What would you like me to do?"

"Will you play and sing for us? I was supposed to perform for our guests, but I've developed a very scratchy throat. I'm afraid that I'm catching cold." Emily coughed, rather unconvincingly. "I've already spoken to Mama, and she thinks it a splendid idea."

"I would much rather not," replied Dorinda hastily, casting a reproachful glance at Letty who seemed about to burst with mirth. "I'm sure that there must be many ladies present tonight who sing and play much better than I do."

"Not I, certainly," said Letty with a giggle. "You've heard *me* sing, Dorinda."

"I'm sorry to hear that you have a cold, Emily," said the duke gently. "It came on very suddenly, I gather?" He turned to Dorinda, amusement lurking behind his eyes. "I'm relieved to hear that you have musical talents, Miss Hayle. I see nothing for it but to implore you to come to our rescue."

Dreading the thought of making herself conspicuous, Dorinda mounted another weak protest, but was overruled by Letty and Emily who each took an arm and marched her to the pianoforte. While Dorinda pulled off her gloves and settled herself at the instrument, Emily made a pretty speech of introduction, which made Dorinda even more nervous as conversation died away and every eye in the room became fastened to her. Drawing a steadying breath, she played one of Mozart's short rondos. At the conclusion, rising to bow to the audience, she was not disturbed to hear a merely polite applause; she was quite aware that her playing skills were little more than competent.

"I think that's quite enough, Emily," she murmured, preparing to leave the instrument. "Your guests have better things to do than listen to me."

"Oh, no. We shan't let you get away from us that easily," said Emily playfully, catching Dorinda's arm. "Letty and I insist, you must sing that beautiful song that you were playing for us just the other day, 'The Bonny Earl of Murray.'"

Out of the corner of her eye, Dorinda saw Shalford's head lift at the mention of the song title. He moved closer to the pianoforte, and she demurred hastily, "I'm sorry, I don't remember it well enough to play without music."

"Oh, what a bouncer, Dorinda!" teased Letty. "I overheard you singing it to yourself only yesterday."

"Yes, do sing the song, Miss Hayle. It's one of my favorites," said the duke quietly.

Bowing to the inevitable, Dorinda played several soft chords then lifted her high, sweet soprano in the song: " 'Ye *Highlands* and ye *Lawlands*, Oh! where ha'e ye been: They ha'e slain the Earl of *Murray*, And they laid him on the Green. . . .' " When she was singing the last line Dorinda looked up to observe with a sinking heart that Shalford's face had hardened into a black scowl.

Amid a hearty round of applause and cries of "Encore, encore," Dorinda quickly moved away from the pianoforte, murmuring "Thank you's" for the appreciative compliments she was receiving as she passed through the guests, many of whom had never before noticed her as an individual. She made for the door of the drawing room, impelled by an acute sense of panic, and slipped into the hall just as Sir Fabian Mordaunt came up to her, blocking her path.

"Well, my girl, you're quite the actress, aren't you?" he sneered, his hooded eyes smoldering. "That demure, missish air of yours completely fooled me. I never suspected that Lady Letitia Wingate's companion was really a common strumpet from the theatre!"

Casting a haunted glance around her, Dorinda was grateful to perceive that she and Sir Fabian had not yet attracted any curious attention from the handful of guests in the hall. "You're really quite mistaken, Sir Fabian," she said in a low voice. "I'm not a professional actress. If you will just let me explain—"

"What kind of an explanation could there possibly be? I saw you, exhibiting yourself on that stage in Brighton." Sir Fabian's eyes narrowed. "But speaking of explanations, I can't believe that Lady Torrington would knowingly foist someone like you on London Society. I daresay that you've fooled her too, that she doesn't realize who you actually are."

"She doesn't know about my stage appearances, no, but Sir Fabian, you really don't understand the—"

"Oh, I understand well enough, Miss Hayle, and let me tell you it will be both a duty and a pleasure to inform Lady Torrington about the viper that she's been harboring in her bosom. And I shall inform Shalford!" Sir Fabian suddenly laughed in pure glee. "He's been discretion itself, but it's dawned on me recently that he's dangling after Lady Letitia. And since he would never knowingly allow a ladybird to chaperone the young female he expected to marry, he must have been as great a flat as I was, both of us bamboozled by a golden wig and a liberal application of stage paint! How I

shall enjoy seeing his face when he discovers the true identity of Miss Dorinda Hayle!"

Despising the necessity of pleading with this odious man,
Dorinda forced herself to say, "If you would just listen to
me, I think I could persuade you to keep silent about . . .
about what you consider to be my wicked past. I'm not
asking for myself, mind. I'm thinking about Lady Letitia—
how gossip could injure her reputation—and Lady Lionel. I
know that she's a very old friend of yours, and you must see
that a scandal involving Letty and the duke would affect her
too."

Sir Fabian was silent for only a moment. Then he
answered brutally, "That was a good try, but for me even
friendship has its limits. Nobody humiliates me in public as
you did—and as Shalford did—without paying for it. I've
been waiting for months, confident that somehow, some-
time, I would have the opportunity to get back at Shalford
for that little incident at Brighton. But I wasn't so sure
about you. I went back to the theatre, the morning after
your vicious attack on me with the poker, and tried to track
down your whereabouts, but that red-headed actor friend of
yours wouldn't tell me anything about you. I always wondered where you went, how you managed to cover your trail.
I certainly never dreamed that you would turn up in the
company of the greatest names in England!"

From behind Dorinda came Shalford's voice, gritty with
controlled rage. "A word with you, Mordaunt."

Dorinda wondered blankly how she could have forgotten,
if only temporarily, that Shalford, too, had pierced her
disguise; she wondered also for how long he had been listening to her conversation with Sir Fabian.

"I'll talk to you later, Shalford. I haven't yet finished my
chat with Miss Hayle."

The duke grasped Sir Fabian's arm in a steely grip that
made the baronet wince. "This is my house, Mordaunt, and

either you come with me quietly as I ask, or I'll have you thrown off the premises by my servants in the full view of all your friends."

His face twisted with malicious triumph, Sir Fabian jerked his arm away, saying, "I don't choose to brawl with you, sir. I agree to talk with you, but if you imagine that you can persuade me not to expose this . . . this lady, thereby saving you from the public ridicule that you so richly deserve, you are badly mistaken."

"We'll see who's mistaken. Just come along with me to the morning room. I believe that it's unoccupied at the moment." As Shalford turned to walk with Sir Fabian down the hall to the morning room, he paused, wheeling sharply on his heel to say to Dorinda in a soft, icily correct voice, "I would appreciate it if you would hold yourself at my disposal, Miss Hayle. I would like a brief word with you too."

Her stomach contracting into painful knots, Dorinda stood, hesitating, outside the drawing room, knowing she would soon attract curious eyes if she lingered alone in the hallway, but feeling a vast unwillingness to talk to anyone. Finally, bracing her shoulders, she entered the drawing room in the wake of the butler and several footmen who were bringing in the tea trays.

Letty pounced on Dorinda immediately. "Where have you been? Everyone was dying to hear you sing again. Why, Dorinda, you look—Aren't you feeling well?"

"No, I'm not," replied Dorinda, fastening on the excuse immediately. No matter how much it would displease the duke, she decided that she could not face the prospect of an angry talk with him tonight. "I'd like to go home and to bed, Letty. Let me have just a word with Lady Lionel."

Her hostess was solicitous. "My dear girl, of course you mustn't stay a single moment longer. Sit down, and we will take care of everything. Letty, I believe that you will find your grandmother in the library; please tell her that Miss

Hayle has been taken ill and is returning to Berkeley Square. She will send the carriage back for you and Lady Torrington."

Riding back to Torrington House through the dark, empty streets, Dorinda rested her head against the squabs of the carriage and thought bleakly that the time of reckoning had come. Before another twenty-four hours had elapsed, she would undoubtedly be seated in a fast day coach, well on her way to exile in Brighton. All things considered, perhaps she was fortunate that her luck had lasted as long as it had.

Chapter IX

Dorinda closed her book with a snap after she realized that she had read the same paragraph three times running and still could not remember a word of the content. She left her chair to take a restless turn around the morning room, torn between apprehension over her inevitable confrontation with Shalford, which could occur at any moment, and a desire to have the interview over and done with, no matter what the consequences.

She had followed her customary daily routine this morning, rising early for her riding lesson with the groom, Jarrett, but she had derived little pleasure from the outing. Her mind was too full of the debacle of Emily Leyburne's coming-out party the previous evening. At breakfast, lacking her usual hearty appetite, she had managed to choke down only a bit of bread and a cup of tea. Now she waited numbly in the morning room for Shalford's arrival, sure that it would not be long delayed.

"Yes, of course, Frith, show him in," she said when the

butler announced that the duke wished to see her. Shalford
strode purposefully into the room, and Dorinda, waiting
until the butler had bowed himself out, said tautly, "I
apologize for not waiting to talk to you last night as you
requested, but I thought it might be better to delay our
discussion until we both felt calmer."

"Thank you, Miss Hayle, but I've never been in any
danger of losing my composure, and I see no need whatsoever for a discussion," snapped Shalford, the rigidity of his
shoulders and the banked anger behind his eyes belying his
words. "I trust that your portmanteau is packed, strapped,
and ready to go," he continued bitingly, "because after I
talk to Lady Torrington, I guarantee that she will send you
away from this house immediately. However, before that
happens, will you just satisfy my curiosity by telling me how
a prime article from the theatre managed to inveigle herself
into a position with one of the most prominent families in
the country?"

Shalford's contemptuous words had an oddly bracing
effect on Dorinda. Her nervousness dropped away as she
said coldly, "Permit me to tell you that you are dead wrong,
Your Grace, as you so very often are! I'm no professional
actress. That night at the Brighton theatre when we first
met, I had appeared on the stage exactly ten times. I had
agreed to perform in a brief and limited run of *The Lady of
the Lake* because I needed money to support my mother."

"That's a very tired story, Miss Hayle. Try again,"
advised Shalford with a derisive laugh. "I daresay that
you'll be telling me next that your mother was old and ill
and widowed."

Dorinda lifted her chin. "She was recently widowed,
certainly."

Shalford laughed again. He came up to her, placing his
hands on her shoulders, his dark eyes raking her face. "Not
a professional actress? With your voice, your stage pres-

ence? How else could you have transformed yourself from a high flyer, at home to a peg with a song and a dance, to a cultured, demure gentlewoman?"

The smoldering anger in his eyes flared to life, and he clasped her roughly against him, pressing his mouth to hers in a savagely bruising kiss. For a moment—several moments—Dorinda felt herself surrendering to the throbbing enticement of a suddenly aroused physical desire. In revulsion, pushing hard against his chest, she pulled away, reaching up with one hand to strike him across the face with all the strength she could muster.

"There," she exclaimed breathlessly. "That's the second time that I've had to remind you that I'm not one of your bits of muslin."

Stepping back, startled, his hand held to his rapidly reddening cheek, he stared at her almost with disbelief. Then, clenching his fists against the temptation to unleash his freshly aroused fury, he grated, "Oh, let's grant that *I* don't appeal to you, nor does Fabian Mordaunt apparently. But don't try to convince me that you're some poor maligned damsel of spotless purity. Perhaps your taste in men runs more to that actor friend of yours—what's his name, Desmond Barry? I notice that he's acting in London now."

Dorinda ground her teeth together. "No, I'm not Desmond Barry's fancy piece either, Duke. I meant what I said: I appeared on stage for a very brief engagement only, so that I could provide for my mother."

"Oh, so we're back to your aged, widowed mother, are we? My heart bleeds for her, and for you too, forced into the acting life so that you could save the poor lady from starvation. I presume that she was homeless, that she had just been thrown out into the street by a heartless landlord because she had no money to pay the rent."

"No, she wasn't homeless," retorted the goaded Dorinda. "She has a perfectly good lease that won't be up until next

January. And my mother is not old or infirm. As a matter of fact, until a few months ago, she was accustomed to being taken care of in reasonable comfort by a titled husband."

"A titled husband?" exclaimed Shalford incredulously. "I have already noted your inventiveness, but this bit of fantasy surpasses everything."

"Fantasy!" flared Dorinda. "I'll have you know that my mother is the widow of Lord Roger Wingate!" She stopped, guilt-stricken. "I . . . please forget that I said that. Lady Torrington doesn't want the relationship known."

Distracted from his anger, Shalford looked hard at her, his brow knit in thought. "I knew, of course, that there was a younger son," he began slowly. "He was something of a black sheep; there was a rumor that he had married most unwisely. But I hadn't heard anything of him for ages. I thought that he had died years ago, matter of fact, somewhere on the Continent. Lady Torrington certainly never mentioned a recent bereavement, nor was there any notice in the *Times* or the *Morning Post* of Lord Roger's death."

"There was no notice of it because Lady Torrington preferred not to call any attention to Lord Roger's death. To his mother, he had already been as good as dead for many years. His 'unwise marriage,' you see, was to my mother, Charlotte Hayle, a minor actress in provincial repertory."

Shalford raised an incredulous eyebrow. "Lady Torrington knew your identity when she employed you?"

"She did." Feeling strangely composed now that the last of her secrets was out of the Pandora's box of concealment, she went on. "Our lawyer in Brighton had written to her, asking her to continue paying to my mother the allowance that Lady Torrington had granted to Lord Roger. Mr. Stowe, bless him, apparently also wrote some complimentary things about me. Lady Torrington came along to Brighton to have a look at me and ended up engaging me as companion to Lady Letty. As you are aware, she didn't feel that her health would permit her to guide Letty through the season, and there was no one else she could call upon. She—we—felt it would be best not to mention my background."

"A wise decision, but perhaps not a very honest one. Very well then, Miss Hayle, you're not a professional actress. But all the same, it was *not* the correct thing to engage you as Lady Letty's companion. I had thought better of Lady Torrington's judgment. Even if you *are* a family connection—of sorts, that is—should it come out that you had actually appeared on stage, Lady Letty's reputation might be compromised."

Dorinda's voice changed. "Well . . . that's something else again. You see, Lady Torrington doesn't know about my appearances in *the Lady of the Lake*. I've felt guilty about that. I know I should have told her about them before she engaged me."

"Yes, you should." Shalford's voice was cold. "But that's neither here nor there. Now we must plan a way to get out of this scrape with the least chance of harming Lady Letty's reputation." At her quick glance of surprise, he nodded, saying, "I'm not so certain anymore that your dismissal is the best way to handle the situation, Miss Hayle. Your departure might result in the very gossip we are trying to prevent. Perhaps our wisest course is simply to do nothing. Yes, I think that would be best. I won't tell Lady Torrington what I've learned about your stage activities. You will stay on as Lady Letty's companion, and then, at the end of the season, you can leave quietly, go back to Brighton or anywhere you choose." He added savagely, "I, for one, will be heartily glad to see the last of you. And provided you promise to keep away from Lady Letty in future and to engage yourself not to speak of the family connection, I'm prepared to make it well worth your while."

"There will be no need to pay me off, Duke," exploded Dorinda. "I assure you, I won't contaminate Letty, either by my association with her in London or by gossiping about her later."

Shalford shrugged. "As you prefer. That is all we have to say to each other, I believe. I bid you good day, Miss Hayle." Bowing stiffly, he turned to go.

"Good day to you, Your Grace," snapped Dorinda, matching his curtness. Then, as another worry surfaced, she called out, "Wait . . . there's something you've forgotten. Sir Fabian Mordaunt also recognized me last night, you know. He threatened to spread my story all over town."

Shalford paused, hat and stick in hand. "If he told the whole story, he would be the laughing stock of London. I'm referring to your attack on him with the poker, of course. However, such a revelation would make the scandal even worse from our point of view. He doesn't like either of us very much, Miss Hayle, and he was certainly planning to make you a prime target of gossip, via an expurgated version of his meeting with you in Brighton, when I contrived to change his mind."

"Oh . . . how did you do that?"

"It was really quite simple. Oh, there was a bit of excitement just at first. He rather fancies himself with his fives, but it was bellows to mend with him in a few seconds. He'll now have to explain a woefully darkened daylight—that or stay out of company for a day or so."

"I'm not sure that I understand—"

"I beg your pardon. I don't usually employ prizefighting slang in talking with a lady. I meant merely that Mordaunt will be sporting a very black eye for the next few days."

"But won't that make Sir Fabian even more vindictive, more eager to spread the story?" inquired Dorinda anxiously. "I'm sure that he wouldn't be nearly so angry with me for . . . for spurning his advances, if I hadn't also hit him with the poker."

"A knockdown at my hands has undoubtedly fueled

Mordaunt's desire to harm both of us, but fortunately I have other means of persuasion," replied the duke coolly. "Recently, I suspected him of cheating in a game of whist at White's. I said nothing about it at the time because I had no actual proof; since he's the Regent's equerry it would have created all manner of unpleasantness. And, as I've told you, my sister-in-law has always had a lingering fondness for Mordaunt. But last night at my house I told him that unless he agreed to keep silent about you I would mention my suspicions about his cheating to a few of the members at White's: Brummell, Sexton, Alvanley—the most influential members. Mordaunt knows full well that it wouldn't take very long for him to be ostracized by every clubman in London."

"I see. Yes, I imagine such a threat might constrain Sir Fabian."

"There's no 'might' about it. You have my word, it *will* stop Mordaunt in his tracks. And now, if you have nothing further to say? . . . No? Then good day, Miss Hayle."

As she watched Shalford leave the room, Dorinda felt curiously deflated. She knew she ought to be relieved because the threat of being exposed as a former actress was no longer hanging over her head, but she could not banish a depressed feeling that her life had lost its savor. The feeling persisted into the next week, as she dragged herself automatically, almost as though she were sleepwalking, through several engagements every day, without remembering very much about any of them.

"I certainly didn't care for that champagne we had at Lady Lynnfield's the other night, though she said it came from Gunther's," remarked Lady Torrington. She was sitting with Dorinda and Letty in the morning room, making final plans for Letty's ball which would be one of the last events of the season. Dorinda had found herself largely taking over the arrangements from the dowager's ineffectual companion, Miss Minniott. "See Gunther's about it, won't you, Miss Hayle?"

"I'll go there this afternoon. How convenient that they're right across the square from us."

"Let me see now. Letty is to have her final fitting on Friday? Well, I think that covers everything except—oh, did you send an invitation to Letty's other godmother, Lady Ennis? Good. She's been ailing of late—her gout is even worse than mine, and I'm sure that she won't come—but she should be invited." Lady Torrington glanced sharply at her granddaughter. "You haven't opened your mouth since we sat down. I don't even think you've been listening. Aren't you interested in your own ball?"

"Why, of course, Grandmama. But there's no need for me to say anything, surely? You and Dorinda are managing so well."

"You look a little pale, Letty. Miss Hayle, perhaps we should send for Doctor Drayton to give Letty a tonic of some sort. I do believe that all this racketing about has quite worn the child down."

"Oh, Grandmama, I don't need a doctor. I'm not the least bit ill, or run-down. Today I'm a little tired, perhaps. Dorinda and I stayed very late last night at the Duchess of Devonshire's ball. There was such a crush at the end of the evening, waiting for our carriage to arrive. We must have waited for over an hour."

"Well, I still think that you look a little pale, but . . . Mind, I want you to take a nap this afternoon. It doesn't pay to get too tired, Letty. You still have more than two weeks of the season to go, and I don't want you going into a decline before our very eyes."

"A decline!" Letty whooped. "Don't talk fustian, Grandmama. Come now, confess it; you've been secretly reading all those novels by Monk Lewis and Mrs. Radcliffe that you were always warning me against!"

"Yes, and what good did I accomplish by that?" retorted the dowager. "Your governess was forever coming to me, wringing her hands and reporting that she had found *Mysteries of Udolpho* or some such trash hidden away under your mattress."

After Lady Torrington, diverted from her intention to summon a doctor, had left the room, Dorinda looked closely at Letty. She had been too wrapped up in her own depressed feelings during the past few days to pay much attention to Letty's frame of mind, but now that Dorinda thought about it, she realized that her young charge had been uncharacteristically subdued recently.

"You *are* pale, Letty. Are you sure that you don't have a headache?"

"Oh, Dorinda, not you too! No, I don't have a headache, not even a trace of one. How often must I say it, I'm just a bit tired."

Letty sounded petulant, and this departure from her usual sunny good nature sharpened Dorinda's sense that something was wrong. "Very well, you aren't ill, but you *have* seemed out of sorts of late," she persisted. "Perhaps your grandmother is right, you've been overdoing it. There was one day last week when we started out with a breakfast engagement and then didn't have one moment to relax until we tumbled into our beds in the small hours of the next morning."

"Oh, that," said Letty listlessly. "Well, if you'd really like to know, I *am* getting very tired of this interminable season. I can't wait to leave London and get back to Waltham Court."

Dorinda rose and went to sit beside Letty, taking one of her hands. "Is that what's wrong, Letty? You're just bored with your first season and you'd like to get back to the country? Or is there something else?"

Jumping up from her chair, Letty took a restless turn

about the room. "Dorinda, do you think that Grandmama and . . . and the duke would agree to postpone my wedding?" she burst out. "Grandmama keeps speaking of the autumn, or just before Christmas, but that's so soon. Why can't we wait until the spring?"

Dorinda hesitated. She had never actually spoken to Letty about her coming marriage. Certainly she had never asked Letty outright about her feelings for Shalford, although she had assumed from her talks with Lady Torrington that the girl was perfectly agreeable to the marriage even if she had not really thought seriously about it before coming to London. Dorinda said quietly, "Letty, have you been thinking that perhaps you don't wish to marry the duke, after all?"

Letty turned a startled face to Dorinda. "Oh, no. I'm sure that it's a very good match, just what Grandmama wants for me. And I'm . . . I'm fond of the duke. It's just that . . . you see, being Duchess of Shalford means that I'll occupy such an important position. I'll have so many duties, and I'm just not sure I'll be able to carry them out. I think I need to be more grown-up, Dorinda. Sometimes . . . sometimes I feel that I haven't really had a chance to be young yet," Letty finished wistfully.

"Why don't you speak to your grandmother?" Dorinda suggested gently. "She may just say that you have a premature case of wedding jitters, but I'm sure she wouldn't want to rush you into marriage before you're ready. She'll probably be perfectly agreeable to postponing the wedding until next spring."

Privately, however, Dorinda was not so sure. It might be that Letty wanted to postpone her wedding simply because, as she had indicated, she was frightened at the prospect of becoming one of the most prominent society hostesses in England. It might also be that Letty, perhaps without realizing it herself, yearned for the romance and excitement of a genuine love match, for it seemed clear to Dorinda that however "fond" Letty might be of the duke, she was not madly in love with him. But neither of these reasons was likely to carry any weight with the dowager. Lady Torrington would probably resist any attempt on Letty's part to postpone or to back out of the Shalford marriage; in the dowager's day, suitability, not romance, was the only criterion for a good match.

"I suppose that I might mention a spring wedding date to Grandmama," replied Letty rather doubtfully. She managed a sudden forced little smile. "Yes, that's just what I'll do. And look, Dorinda, will you forgive me for inflicting my fit of megrims on you? I daresay that you're right, that I'm overly tired; and perhaps I do have—what did you call it?— a case of wedding jitters. I feel much better now that I've talked to you."

With this, Dorinda had to be satisfied. But she continued to be concerned about Letty's state of mind, especially when, later in the afternoon, the girl opted for a carriage ride in Hyde Park rather than the brisk canter on horseback in which she usually delighted. During the drive, Letty remained quiet and abstracted, often failing to return a friend's greeting until reminded to do so by a quick nudge from Dorinda.

Shalford rode up to their carriage soon after they had passed through the gates of the park, greeting Letty with his customary smiling solicitude. "What a fetching hat. I don't believe I've seen it before," he exclaimed, admiring Letty's demure poke bonnet with the cherry ribbons that brought out the color in her cheeks and matched the fabric of her dress of jaconet muslin.

To Dorinda, as had been the case since their furious quarrel on the morning after Emily's party, he extended a greeting so coldly correct that it came within a hairbreadth of being a direct snub. She suppressed a quick pang of hurt

mingled with anger, reminding herself that it did not matter
what Shalford's opinion of her might be, provided he kept
his silence and allowed her to finish out her engagement
with Lady Torrington.

"I understand that Drury Lane will mount a revival of
The Count of Narbonne next week," Shalford now
remarked to Letty. "Would you like to attend a performance? Shall I make up a party?"

The invitation, so clearly aimed at Letty's passion for the
supernatural and the melodramatic, brought only a subdued
thanks from her and the statement, "Perhaps we could let
you know later? I don't remember exactly what Grandmama has planned for us next week."

"Certainly. Just as you wish. I'm completely at your
disposal." Despite his cool reply, Shalford was plainly taken
back. Narrowing his eyes, he directed a long, hard look at
Dorinda. However, he said nothing more on the subject
before taking his leave. "Good day, Lady Letty, Miss Hayle.
I hope to see you at Carlton House on Friday."

"I'm a little surprised that you didn't snatch at the opportunity to see *The Count of Narbonne*," ventured Dorinda
after the duke had left. "I recall that you liked the book
upon which it is based, Mr. Walpole's *Castle of Otranto,* so
very much."

"I did enjoy the book, but really, Dorinda, don't you think
the story is rather childish? Here we have a ghost who
grows, becoming so enormous thàt his ancestral castle won't
hold him any longer so he tears it down!"

Dorinda had scarcely had time to digest such heresy from
Letty when she was further jolted by the arrival alongside
their carriage of Peregrine Lacey and Sir Fabian Mordaunt.
It was a totally unlikely pairing—Dorinda would have supposed that Perry and Sir Fabian were, at most, nodding
acquaintances—but they seemed to be on excellent terms.
Sir Fabian paid Letty his usual compliments, and he greeted

Dorinda civilly enough, but as his swift hate-filled glance raked her face, she was sure that his fury and resentment, though rendered futile by Shalford's intervention, were still very much alive.

Noting with considerable satisfaction the sickly green and yellow areas around Sir Fabian's right eye, Dorinda inquired sweetly, "I see that you have injured your eye, sir. I do hope that it is not too painful?"

"Not at all. I'm quite on the way to recovery. But thank you for your interest." Sir Fabian had managed to reply with commendable restraint, but a flash in his eyes told her what his reply would have been had they been alone.

"Yes. Sir Fabian ran into a door," chortled Perry. "We've all been urging him to be very careful of doors in the future. Some fight back, eh, Mordaunt?" Paying no attention to Sir Fabian's wan response to his raillery, Perry rushed on. "Guess what, Letty, Miss Hayle. Sir Fabian has nominated me to the Four-in-Hand Club. I'm to go on my first run with them on Sunday. You know the routine, I fancy. We assemble in George Street and then drive to Salt Hill—very steady driving, no coach allowed to pass another, the pace never to exceed a trot. At Salt Hill we have dinner at the Windmill before returning to London. By Jove, I can't tell you how much I'm looking forward to it!" Perry's expressive face clouded. "Of course, my horses are well enough, but they're nothing to Lord Barrymore's matched bays. I don't suppose that I'll ever drive as well as he does, either."

"I'm sure that you'll measure up, Perry," Letty comforted him. "Sir Fabian wouldn't have nominated you to the Club if he doubted your driving ability. Isn't that so, Sir Fabian?"

Sir Fabian instantly agreed and Perry recovered his sunny disposition, but after the two men had ridden on Letty remarked anxiously, "I hadn't realized that Perry had become so friendly with that man. I cannot like it. Everyone knows that Sir Fabian is a notorious gambler. The *on-dit* is that he's quite run off his legs, that he's in the clutches of the cents-per-cent. Dorinda, you don't suppose that he will persuade Perry to join him at the gambling tables out of gratitude for being put up for the Four-in-Hand Club?"

"I shouldn't worry. Mr. Lacey has never shown any liking for gambling in the past, has he? And you know how much he has always longed to be nominated to the Four-in-Hand Club," replied Dorinda soothingly. But, on the drive home from the park, she acknowledged to herself that she shared Letty's anxieties for her childhood friend. Dorinda could understand why the volatile, impressionable Perry would be flattered by the attentions of a much older man who occupied a distinguished position in society. But why had Sir Fabian suddenly become interested in Perry? Could it be that there was some connection between this newly developed friendship and Sir Fabian's frustrated urge to revenge himself on Dorinda? Try as she might, Dorinda could not fathom what that connection might be.

Chapter X

Dorinda took the breakfast tray from the footman and sat down with her tea and toast at a small table in her bedchamber, feeling rather sinfully indolent. It was already past ten, and she had not yet stirred from her room. Thinking she had not risen so late of a morning since her arrival at Torrington House, she smiled to herself. There was really no reason to feel slothful. Last night had been the occasion of Letty's coming-out ball, and Dorinda had not been able to sink into bed until the first streaks of sunrise had appeared on the horizon. Long after Lady Torrington and Letty had retired, long after the last guest had sought his carriage, Dorinda, in alliance with Frith, and the housekeeper had supervised the house servants and the extra workers hired for the night as they labored to put the house to rights after what had been universally acclaimed as *the* event of the season.

"I fancy that we've surpassed ourselves, my dear," Lady Torrington had remarked complacently to Dorinda, and the dowager was quite right. Everyone who *was* anyone had been there, including the Prince Regent and Beau Brummell, who had carefully avoided each other all evening; they were no longer on speaking terms. Due to the crush there had been insufficient room to move on the dance floor. At least five ladies had fainted and more than a dozen expensive gowns had been so damaged by rips and spills that they could never be worn again. Outside in the street, where departing guests awaited their carriages, there had been two collisions and numerous altercations between drivers. But the food and wines had been superb, the orchestra sheer perfection, and everyone had agreed that Letty had never seemed so beautiful.

. . . Or so radiant, thought Dorinda. She paused with her teacup halfway to her lips, thinking about Letty's behavior at the ball. The moping, listless girl of the past several weeks had reverted to her normal bright self. She had danced every dance, traded outrageous jokes with Peregrine Lacey, teased Emily Leyburne about her numerous beaux, and managed to sneak several glasses of champagne under the disapproving eye of her grandmother. Once, having caught Dorinda alone, she had said with a rather surprising intensity, "Thank you for putting up with all my moods. I'm going to be very happy from now on, you'll see."

There had been another very happy person at the ball last night. Adelaide Caldecott, her eyes shining with a soft glow, had sought out Dorinda, saying, "It isn't to be announced yet, but I wanted you to know that Sir Fabian and I are to be married." The bedazzled baroness had apparently failed to notice that Dorinda's words of felicitation were little more than lukewarm.

If Shalford had been pleased by his future financée's return to her usual good spirits, he had given no indication of his pleasure to Dorinda. He had not, in fact, even deigned to speak to her at the ball. He had merely directed at her from across the room the briefest of cold nods.

Her appetite suddenly gone, Dorinda put down her slice of toast. Why should she care, she demanded of herself, if the duke persisted in his attitude of unforgiving hostility? In a few days, the season would be over, and she would be free to return to Eastfield where she need never again worry about keeping Letty out of mischief, or about the danger of having her stage background revealed to Lady Torrington, or about the necessity of maintaining at least a guarded truce with His Grace the Duke of Shalford.

Dorinda's shoulders slumped. A few short months ago she would have viewed the prospect of living quietly in Eastfield, with her own and her mother's financial future secured, if not with feelings of overwhelming happiness, at least with a sense of contentment and relief. Now she found herself looking toward a future that suddenly seemed unaccountably bleak. She realized that she would miss the excitement and vitality of London life. She would miss the stimulating company of the high-born and influential people she had met here. She would miss Letty whom she had grown to love almost as a younger sister. And she would miss . . . Dorinda rose hastily, banishing from her mind that last perverse, disturbing, utterly illogical feeling, and refusing even to admit the possibility that she could ever miss the wilful, infuriating presence of the Duke of Shalford.

Leisurely, she began to dress, donning a sprigged muslin in pale blue and trying out the effect of a new hair arrangement. There was no need to hurry because Lady Torrington had not scheduled any engagements for Letty on the day after her ball, being certain she would rise much later than her usual hour. Dorinda glanced at her watch. It was after eleven. Surely even the slugabed Letty would not sleep much longer. Dorinda left her bedchamber, walked down the corridor to Letty's room, and tapped lightly on the door. Receiving no answer, she opened the door quietly and peered inside the room. Letty's large canopied bed faced the door, but Letty was not in it. Feeling a quick flurry of alarm, Dorinda walked into the bedchamber. The room was empty. From the appearance of the smooth counterpane, Letty had not slept in the bed. Her lovely white ball gown had been thrown carelessly over a chair, and the door of the wardrobe was open, revealing a number of garments that had been dragged out hurriedly and then imperfectly replaced on their hangers. A small portmanteau—discarded because a large size was needed?—stood open on the floor. There was no evading the truth: Letty had run away. After a moment of numbed disbelief, Dorinda walked to the desk, looking for a farewell note, a letter of explanation. There was none, not on the desk or anywhere else in the room.

Still dazed, Dorinda stood, indecisive, for a moment longer; then she crossed the room to the bell rope. To the young footman who answered her ring, she said, "Please ask Betsy Morris to come to Lady Letitia's bedchamber." The footman returned to say, wooden-faced, "Betsy Morris doesn't seem to be anywhere in the house, miss."

Dorinda sat down heavily. So, she would get no information from Betsy; Letty's abigail had accompanied her mistress. But where—and why—had they gone? Surely not to Letty's beloved Waltham Court, the Wingate country seat. In a very few days, with the season ended, Letty would have been going there as a matter of course with her grandmother. Certainly she had not gone anywhere with Shalford. The duke would never seek to compromise his future wife. Unwillingly, Dorinda's thoughts admitted another name. Could Letty have gone off with Desmond Barry? But that seemed impossible. It had been weeks since Letty had seen Desmond, so far as Dorinda knew, or even mentioned his name. And Dorinda in her heart of hearts had never really believed that Letty felt anything for Desmond except friendship, perhaps mingled with envy of his unconventional and adventurous way of life.

At length Dorinda rose. Speculation was useless, but she believed with bone-deep conviction that she would soon know where Letty had gone. Impulsive and unthinking the girl might be, but there was no hint of cruelty or meanness in her character. Sooner—and Dorinda fervently prayed that it would be sooner—or later, Letty would send word of her whereabouts. Picking up the filmy ball dress, Dorinda hung it in the wardrobe, placed the small portmanteau on a shelf, and closed the doors of the piece. Now, to a casual observer, it would not be obvious that Letty had packed some of her belongings and left Torrington House.

Too restless, too tightly strung, to remain in her own bedchamber or in Letty's, Dorinda went down the stairs and wandered into the library, picked up several books and put them down again, and then walked into the drawing room. There she sat down at the pianoforte, seeking release from anxiety and tension in the music that had always given her such pleasure.

" 'Ye *Highlands* and ye *Lawlands,* Oh! where ha'e ye been: They ha'e slain the Earl of *Murray,* And they laid him on the Green,' " she found herself singing softly. But she broke off, flushing with vexation. Her fingers shifted into an Elizabethan ballad that her mother had often sung: " 'All in a garden green Two lovers sat at ease, As they could scarce be seen, Among the leafy trees.' "

"Well, my dear, you sound very sprightly, I'm glad to hear. I marvel that you have the energy to play and sing after your long night. Frith tells me that you didn't go up to your bed until sunrise."

Dorinda turned toward the dowager. "Oh . . . yes. I thought that Frith and the housekeeper might like some assistance in putting the house to rights after the ball. But if Frith felt that I was interfering in any way—"

"Do not be concerned, Miss Hayle. Frith had nothing but praise for you." Lady Torrington, clad in pelisse and bonnet,

and obviously on her way to an engagement, sat down near
Dorinda. "Where is that scamp, Letty? Still not awake?"

"Not yet. It was a very long and tiring night for her,
though I'm sure she enjoyed it immensely," replied Dorinda,
wondering grimly if there was the slightest possibility that
Letty's disappearance could be kept from the dowager.

"Don't bother your head about that either," laughed
Lady Torrington. "I never saw the chit enjoy herself more."
She narrowed her eyes at Dorinda. "I was going to talk to
you a little later, Miss Hayle, but it may as well be now.
Shalford and I had a discussion last night. He would like me
to announce his betrothal to Letty next month and set the
wedding date for just before Michaelmas. Of course, I gave
him my approval, but, quite frankly, I don't think that my
health will stand up to planning a wedding on such a scale as
this one must be. Fanny Minniott would help, but . . . poor
Fanny, I fear that she isn't very competent. However, *you*
are, Miss Hayle. Would you consider staying on after the
season to take the arrangements for Letty's wedding off my
shoulders?"

"Could I think about it for a bit, Lady Torrington?"
Dorinda asked after a moment. Suddenly the prospect of
planning a splendid wedding for Letty and Shalford seemed
infinitely depressing. And with Letty missing, there was a
very good chance that the wedding would never take place
at all. "My mother expects me back at the beginning of
August. She's been growing increasingly lonely without
me."

The dowager frowned. "Lonely? But doesn't she have
friends and neighbors in Eastfield? In the natural course of
events, a mother cannot plan on keeping her child with her
forever. What would"—Lady Torrington obviously found it
difficult to give Charlotte Wingate her proper title—"what
would Lady Roger do, for example, if you had the opportunity to marry? Not that it's very likely, of course, but—you

see, I had it in mind to ask you to take over not just the preparations for Letty's wedding but other duties as well. How would you like to be my companion, Miss Hayle? Fanny Minniott is getting old and forgetful and beyond the demands of the position. I propose to pension her off and replace her with someone younger and more capable."

Dorinda had to repress an impulse to giggle. In view of the dowager's initial opinion of her son's stepdaughter, it was ironic that Lady Torrington now wished to keep Dorinda in her household permanently. For an instant, Dorinda contemplated a future spent constantly in the dowager's dominating presence. It would be insupportable, of course, but there would be the opportunity to enjoy Letty's company occasionally and to . . . She tore her mind away from such treacherous thoughts, back to reality. "Thank you for your flattering offer. May I think about that too?"

The dowager departed for her luncheon party, mildly displeased that Dorinda had not accepted with alacrity the position as her companion. Left to herself, without the distraction of Lady Torrington's presence, Dorinda was free to fret about Letty's disappearance. Mercifully, fate inflicted on her only another hour of uncertainty. Shortly after noon the butler Frith brought her a note addressed in a familiar untidy scrawl. Dorinda's fingers trembled as she tore open the note, for she was certain the contents spelled disaster.

"My darling Dorinda," Desmond began. "I hope that you won't hate me too much for breaking my word to you. I know that I promised not to see Lady Letty again, but there—I confess it—I'm a flesh and blood man, not a saint, and circumstances have just been too much for me. You may recall that I haven't been satisfied with the roles that John Kemble has been giving me at Covent Garden. At this rate, it will be years before I become a principal player. So recently, when I received an offer from a visiting colonial manager to join a company making a tour of Canada, I accepted. And when Lady Letty begged me to take her along, I agreed to do that, too. Have you realized that the girl has been very unhappy? She doesn't want to marry the Duke of Shalford. I don't know that she really wants to marry me either, but she certainly prefers me to the duke, and I think we can be quite happy together. I always said she was a taking little thing, and of course, when she turns twenty-one, she will have a handsome fortune.

"Break the news to Lady Torrington about her new grandson-in-law at your leisure. There's nothing that the old lady can do to stop us; by the time you receive this note, Letty and I will be halfway to Bristol and our ship. Please don't think too harshly of me, my love. If the situation had been just a little different, it might be you and I starting off to a new life in the New World. I remain, whatever the future has in store for us, your ever devoted Desmond."

Crumbling the note between her palms, Dorinda sat, torn between rage and grief. How could Desmond, for all his careless, vagabond ways, have taken such callous advantage of a very young girl? And how much happiness could this ill-matched pair expect to find when, as was obvious from Desmond's letter and from Dorinda's observations of them, they shared only a mild affection for each other? It was clear now that Dorinda had misinterpreted Letty's mood of the evening before. It was not happiness that Letty had been feeling, but rather a strong sense of relief because she had made the decision to escape the Shalford marriage by eloping with Desmond. Dorinda berated herself for not understanding the depth of Letty's misery. If she had known ... but no. There was little that Dorinda could have done to affect the situation, except to give Letty her sympathy and love and to advise her to confess to her grandmother that she did not wish to marry the duke. Useless advice, because Letty knew quite well that Lady Torrington would never consent, without much rage and travail, to break off such an advantageous alliance.

Dorinda drew a deep breath, straightened her shoulders, and walked purposefully up the stairs to her bedchamber. There she pulled a small portmanteau from the wardrobe and began methodically to pack in it the clothes and toilet articles that she would need for an absence of one, or possibly two, days. Now that she knew what had happened to Letty, she must do what she could, even if the attempt proved useless, to rescue the girl from her folly. As Dorinda packed, her mind busily calculated her chances for success. How far was the port of Bristol? Well over a hundred miles, surely. Desmond and Letty had a very long head start. They had left Torrington House early in the morning, probably before the servants had risen, perhaps only a short time after Letty had said good-bye to her guests and retired to her room. And they had undoubtedly traveled by fast—and expensive—post chaise and four, to lessen the possibility of successful pursuit by the dowager.

As Dorinda closed the portmanteau, she paused. How much would the journey to Bristol and the return cost? Fifty, sixty pounds? More than that probably, when one included generous tips to the postilions. Dorinda did not have that amount of money. And even without the problem of funds, how was her absence, and Letty's—even if they were lucky and returned within two days—to be explained? After a moment's thought, Dorinda wrote a short note and rang for a footman to take it around to Peregrine Lacey's lodgings in Mount Street. Returning rather more quickly than Dorinda could have hoped, the footman brought a discouraging message. According to Cornet Lacey's valet, the young officer was not expected back in his rooms until late afternoon, when he would return to dress for an engagement at White's that evening.

Dorinda allowed herself only a momentary feeling of

defeat. She should have guessed that Perry would not be home. His military duties were not especially onerous, but he still had to spend some time with his regiment. At any rate it was unlikely that he would have had any large sum of money to loan to Dorinda. Perry was improvident at best, and his only source of income was his slender pay.

Knitting her brow briefly, Dorinda again sat down at her desk to pen a careful note to Lady Torrington. Then, having rung for the butler, she handed him the letter, saying, "Please see that Lady Torrington gets this as soon as she comes in. I've just received word that a dear friend of mine has become ill, and I've promised to stay with her tonight, and possibly tomorrow night, until her mother can arrive to take care of her. During my absence, Lady Letitia will be staying with Lady Lionel Leyburne. I've explained all this to Lady Torrington in my letter."

"I'm very sorry to hear about your friend's illness, Miss Hayle. I trust that she will be well soon." The butler spotted Dorinda's portmanteau and picked it up. "I'll just take this downstairs and have one of the footmen hail you a hackney cab."

"Thank you, Frith." Dorinda breathed a short sigh of relief at passing the first hurdle. Apparently Frith had found nothing untoward in her hastily concocted cover story, and perhaps the dowager, who seldom bothered herself with Letty's minute-by-minute activities, would accept the—one hoped—very brief absence of Dorinda and Letty without fuss or curiosity. Frith might wonder why he had not actually seen Letty depart for her stay with Lady Lionel, but he was not likely to communicate his misgivings to Lady Torrington.

Arriving in Cavendish Square a little later, Dorinda found Lady Lionel and Emily about to leave the house. After a quick look at Dorinda's face, Lady Lionel said to Emily, "Go write a little note to Mrs. Northcote, my dear, expressing our regrets at not being able to take tea with her, and have it sent around at once. Miss Hayle, won't you come with me to the morning room?"

"I'm very sorry to be the cause of your missing your engagement," said Dorinda a few minutes later, as she sat tensely upright in her chair.

"Not at all, my dear. I could see that you were distressed. Now, what can I do to help you?"

"Could you possibly loan me sixty pounds—no, perhaps eighty would be better—immediately?" blurted Dorinda.

Lady Lionel's face turned blank from incomprehension. "That's rather a large sum of money," she began slowly. "I don't believe that I have that much in cash in the house . . . but, of course, if you really need it, Miss Hayle, I can get it for you."

Even as Lady Lionel spoke, Dorinda realized that her original plan, which was to keep Letty's elopement a secret from everyone, was unworkable. Even though a bewildered Lady Lionel seemed willing, with no questions asked, to give Dorinda the money she needed to pursue Desmond and Letty, there remained the dangerous possibility that Lady Lionel would unwittingly give the game away if she chanced to encounter Lady Torrington during the next several days.

"Lady Lionel, I'm going to put myself entirely in your hands," Dorinda said with the calm of desperation. "I need this large sum of money to attempt to prevent Letty from ruining her life. I . . . I don't know of any gentle way to break the news to you: Letty has eloped with Desmond Barry, an actor friend of mine. They left early this morning for Bristol. I've left a note for Lady Torrington, saying that Letty will be staying with you for several days while I visit a sick friend. It's not a very original story, but I think that it might just hold water if you will cooperate with me. If I leave London immediately by the fastest means of travel— chaise and four—there is some chance that I can overtake

Letty before she boards ship with Desmond so I can persuade her to come back with me."

"Letty has eloped? With an actor?" Lady Lionel seemed dazed. "I've suspected for some time now that she and Justin weren't very well suited. She's so very young—I've often thought that she acted even younger than her age—and Justin, you know, has always been attracted to poised, self-confident older women—many of them completely ineligible, of course, already married, or not . . . not quite respectable." Blushing, Lady Lionel hurriedly left the subject of Shalford's past dalliances. "But to think that Letty dislikes Justin so much that she would run away with . . . with an actor!"

The identity of Letty's partner seems to be more shocking to Lady Lionel than the actual fact of the elopement, thought Dorinda grimly. Society would certainly concur.

"I don't think that Letty dislikes the duke," replied Dorinda quietly. "I think she's quite fond of him, actually. And I'm fairly sure she doesn't love Desmond, or he her. But she *is* young, as you said—young and immature. Recently I've discovered that she is terrified of assuming the responsibilities attendant on the position of Duchess of Shalford. I'm confident that if I can just talk to her, I can bring her to her senses. I shouldn't be at all surprised to find she is already regretting what she's done."

Lady Lionel gave herself a little shake. "Of course you must go after Letty," she said firmly. "She must be brought back before there is any hint of scandal. But you mustn't go alone. I shall come with you. If you will just give me a few minutes to throw some necessities into a valise . . ."

"Thank you, Lady Lionel, but you can't go with me. You must stay here to provide Letty with an alibi for her grandmother." Appalled, Dorinda drew in a breath. "I've overlooked something else. The duke will certainly wonder where Letty is, and we can't very well tell him that she's staying in his own house!" She knit her brow in fierce concentration. "I have it. You can tell him that Letty refused to allow me to go alone to care for my friend. He won't like that, but he will probably accept it."

"Miss Hayle, I will be happy to help you in any way that I can to extricate Letty from this dreadful situation without scandal," began Lady Lionel slowly. "But even if—I suppose I should say when—you accomplish this, it wouldn't be fair to Justin to keep from him the fact that the girl he wishes to marry had tried to elope with another man."

"The important thing is to get Letty back unharmed and without loss of reputation. Then, if it turns out that she does indeed love the duke but is simply too young and unsure of herself to get married until a later date, there might be no need to tell him anything at all," argued Dorinda.

"I shouldn't wish to risk Justin's happiness . . . if there is any chance of saving it," said Lady Lionel doubtfully, "but I don't like to keep anything from him, either. I suppose we can discuss it again after Letty comes back . . . meanwhile we're wasting time. You must leave immediately. I'll give you a draft on my bank, and—yes, I must be adamant on this point: I cannot permit you to go alone—you must take along one of my maids as a companion. It simply is not done, Miss Hayle; a lady of quality does not travel alone by post chaise."

"I hadn't thought of that either. It *would* raise eyebrows, wouldn't it, if I charged breakneck across England by myself. I'd be happy to have one of your maids as a traveling companion. But I should like to get started as soon as possible, Lady Lionel. Time is all-important. I must reach Letty before she boards ship with Desmond."

Later, standing in the courtyard of the Swan with Two Necks, the bustling coaching inn in Gresham Street, Dorinda glanced at her watch with some satisfaction. It had taken less time than she had imagined to make a stop at

Lady Lionel's bank and to engage a chaise and four at the Swan with Two Necks. But it was already slightly past two o'clock, and Letty and Desmond had a start of many hours. She had heard that post horses, on toll roads and in good weather conditions, could achieve a speed of ten or even twelve miles an hour. But even so, and even if she paused at each posting house only long enough to change teams, it would be difficult to make up much time on the long journey to Bristol. She must hope that Desmond would be obliged to wait at least a day or two for his ship to Canada.

"We're ready for you, ma'am," said the hostler, extending a hand to help Dorinda and the maid, Marie, into the chaise as the postboys doffed the white smocks covering their blue uniforms and climbed into their saddles. Trotting smartly, the horses drew the chaise through the busy streets, past St. Paul's, down Ludgate Hill to the Strand and on to Hyde Park Corner and the start of the journey to the west.

Afterward Dorinda could not remember many details of that interminable, bone-wearying trip. The towns flashed by anonymously: Brentford, Stough, Burnham, Maidenhead, Twyford. As they approached each coach stop, a postilion would blow a blast on his long horn, and almost before the chaise had pulled into the courtyard of the inn, a new team was being led out, with the postboys already mounted. At Reading, some forty miles from London, Dorinda and the maid Marie climbed gratefully down from the chaise to enter the inn for a cup of tea and a plate of cold meat in one of the private parlors. As she paid her shot, Dorinda asked to see the proprietor.

"I wonder if you can tell me, sir, if my brother and his wife have passed through here," Dorinda asked, embroidering her remarks freely. "He's a tall, red-headed gentleman, and his wife is petite and pretty and very young. I've just received word, you see, that my mother is very ill in Bath. I greatly fear that she is on her deathbed. I know that my brother was also notified of Mama's illness, and I'm sure that he will do his best to come to her before the end. It would comfort me so much to learn that Richard is already on his way."

"I can certainly understand that, ma'am. I don't recall seeing a gentleman of that description myself, but let me just inquire in the stables." A few minutes later the proprietor reported that a red-headed gentleman and a pretty young woman had indeed changed horses at the inn earlier in the day, in late morning. "He was in a tearing hurry, ma'am, wouldn't stop for refreshments, used dreadful bad language, I'm told, when the hostlers didn't change teams quick enough to suit him."

So, thought Dorinda, as her chaise pulled out of the coaching inn in Reading, Desmond is in a "tearing hurry." She had suspected from the first that he had persuaded Letty not to leave a note of explanation in her bedchamber in order to prevent Dorinda from responding earlier. Knowing Dorinda as he did, Desmond had probably been certain that, rather than notify Lady Torrington about the elopement, Dorinda, in the hope of averting a scandal, would attempt to pursue Letty. He had effectively delayed that pursuit by having his farewell note delivered many hours after he and Letty had left London.

At each stop after Reading, Dorinda asked the same question and received the same answer: A red-haired gentleman and a young lady had passed through, never stopping to rest or eat, always urging the postilions to ever greater speed. Obviously Desmond feared that someone was hot on his trail, and by pushing his horses to their limits, he was insuring that any pursuer could not make up what now appeared to be a six- or seven-hour lead. And Desmond was right, Dorinda reflected dejectedly. There was no possibility of catching up with him and Letty on the road to Bristol; her only hope was that they would meet with a delay in finding a ship, a not unlikely occurrence in view of the recently declared war between England and the United States, and the danger to British shipping from American privateers.

At Hungerford, though the midsummer sun was still shining brightly, Dorinda faced the fact that it was already past eight o'clock, and she and Marie might not have the strength to continue on to Bristol unless they stopped here for some kind of meal and a short rest. After arranging with the landlord of the Red Lion for the use of a bedchamber for several hours and for the provision of a light supper, Dorinda paused on her way to the private dining parlor to ask her oft-repeated question. She was jolted to hear the landlord's cheerful reply: "A red-haired gentleman, ma'am? Why, yes indeed, he stopped here. Matter of fact, he's still here, having himself a fine dinner in my best parlor."

"My brother is here? How wonderful," said Dorinda in a hollow voice. "If you'll just show me which room he is in . . . Thank you. Marie, please go on into the parlor without me and start your meal."

Without bothering to knock, Dorinda pushed open the door of the room indicated by the landlord and walked in. There, sprawled comfortably in an armchair before a table littered with the remains of a lavish dinner, sat Desmond Barry in the act of downing a glass of wine.

"Ah, there you are, my love," he said affably. "You're in very good time."

Chapter XI

Dorinda cast a quick gaze around the parlor. Desmond was obviously its only occupant. "Where is Lady Letitia?" she demanded.

"I have no idea. I haven't seen Lady Letty in weeks, nor am I in the least interested in knowing her whereabouts."

"You're lying, Desmond. At every stage since Reading, I've been told that a red-haired gentleman accompanied by a young lady had stopped to change horses."

"Well, that's true enough. The red-haired gentleman was certainly me, and the young lady was my landlady's daughter. She's a very pretty little piece, by the way, if a trifle empty-headed. She's having a meal in the kitchen right now and will soon be on her way home to London."

"Your landlady's daughter! But . . . you said in your letter that you were eloping with Letty. Why did you lie? And where *is* Letty?" Dorinda clasped her hands together in sudden fear. "She left Torrington House very early this morning with her abigail. If she didn't go off with you, then what has happened to her?"

Rising, Desmond came around the table to put a comforting arm around Dorinda. "Don't bother your beautiful head about Lady Letty. I've no doubt that she's perfectly safe," he said, smiling down at her. "Do come and sit down over here. I have something important to tell you."

The bewildered Dorinda allowed herself to be settled into a chair next to the table. "The only possible subject of importance is Letty's well-being. Are you going to tell me where she is?"

"I've already told you, I don't know where the girl is," replied Desmond impatiently. "Not exactly, anyway. But she's come to no harm, I'm sure of that. Look, Dorinda, forget about Lady Letty for the moment. I want to talk about you and me. You see, as I told you in my letter, I've received a splendid offer to make a tour of Canada. I decided to accept it, but I didn't want to go without you, so—"

Dorinda interrupted him. "Without me?" she said in surprise. "But why would you expect me to go off to Canada with you?"

Desmond eyed her reproachfully. "How can you ask that? You know how I've felt about you from the moment I first saw you, that day I called on you and Lady Roger in Brighton. I'd been counting on joining you at your home in Eastfield after your engagement with Lady Torrington ended next month, as we'd agreed the last time we met."

"As we agreed! Desmond, I said merely that I would be happy to have you visit us when I returned to Eastfield."

"Well, I wasn't sure that I could persuade you to go with me," Desmond continued, ignoring her remark. "So I decided to trick you into following me out of London by allowing you to think that I had eloped with Lady Letty. I knew that you would come tearing after me if you thought that your ewe lamb was in danger, and I was right. It was rather a nice touch, don't you think, taking along my landlady's daughter? You were bound to ask after me at some of the posting stops, where you would be told that I had a young woman with me. What else could you think but that the girl was Lady Letty?"

As Desmond paused to smile with smug satisfaction, Dorinda gazed at him in dazed bewilderment. Even her worries about Letty were forgotten temporarily as she struggled to understand what Desmond was saying. She had the feeling that the connecting parts of his conversation, those that made sense, had been lost, perhaps through inattentiveness on her part, so that she was in the position of attempting to fit together a puzzle with some of the pieces missing. She said carefully: "Let me understand you, Desmond. You accepted an offer to go to Canada, and you wanted me to accompany you. So, without speaking to me first, without giving me the opportunity to say yes or no, you tricked me into following you by pretending to elope with Letty. Do you really expect me to believe a story like that?"

"Well, if I *had* asked you, would you have gone with me?"

"No, of course not. You know very well that Mama's whole future depends on my fulfilling my obligation to Lady Torrington to chaperone Letty through the London season."

"But that's just it, Dorinda, the season will be over in a few days. The old harridan surely can't say that you haven't fulfilled your obligation, now can she?"

Dorinda shook her head in exasperation. "That's neither here nor there. Even if the season were over, I wouldn't have agreed to go with you, Desmond. I don't love you enough to marry you, or to be your doxy, or whatever it is you have in mind. And what's more, I don't think that you love me, either!"

"Now wait, Dorinda. You know that I've spent every

waking moment trying to fix your interest since you joined our company in Brighton."

"Trying to seduce me, you mean," shrugged Dorinda. "But it doesn't signify. I don't pretend to understand why you hatched this mad scheme, Desmond, and I'm not going to try. Now that I know that Letty hasn't been foolish enough to fall into your clutches, I can return to London and forget that I wasted time and money chasing you across half the breadth of England for no good reason." She rose, picking up her reticule and adjusting her bonnet, and headed for the door.

"I don't think that you really want to do that, Dorinda."

Dorinda turned, struck by the note of menace in Desmond's voice. "What? . . . Of course I want to return to London."

Desmond looked at his watch. "Several hours ago Lady Torrington received a note from you saying that you and I had eloped. I daresay you could tell her you had changed your mind about eloping, but would she believe you? Recall, even if you leave here immediately, you won't get back to London until morning. Face it, my dear, your reputation is in shreds. Much better to cut your losses and come with me."

Dorinda withered Desmond with a look of weary disdain. "You're wrong, you know. Lady Lionel Leyburne can prove that I didn't elope with you. Oh, yes"—she nodded as Desmond's expression changed—"I had to tell Lady Lionel the whole story so that I could borrow the money to pay for that very expensive chaise and four. What's more, one of her maids accompanied me on my journey so I'm in no danger of being considered a fallen woman. However, now that you've sent Lady Torrington that malicious note, I won't be able to keep Letty's disappearance from her either. I suppose she'll dismiss me for not taking better care of Letty, but I'd rather take my chances with Lady Torrington than go with you, Desmond. I'm returning to London immediately." Dorinda struck her hands together in a sudden eruption of anxiety. "But what will I tell Lady Torrington when I get there? I still don't know where Letty is."

Desmond, who now sat slumped in his chair, his expression revealing his dejection, lifted his head quickly. "Dorinda, please take my word that Lady Letty has come to no harm. No matter what else I've done, I wouldn't lie to you about a thing like that."

"Then you do know what's happened to her?" asked Dorinda with a sudden flash of hope.

"Well, yes, in a general way—"

"Desmond, please tell me."

Desmond looked harassed. "I can't do that."

"Can't, or won't?"

"Perhaps a little of both. But she's perfectly *all right,* Dorinda. Please don't worry about her. And listen"—he braced his shoulders and tried for a smile—"I admit that it *was* a harebrained scheme, trying to trick you into coming with me. Only . . . I do love you so much, and I thought how wonderful it would be to have you with me in Canada. . . . Won't you forgive me for being such a cloth-head?"

Dorinda eyed Desmond's penitent face and sighed. She remembered his real, if misguided, efforts to help her by giving her a role in his play. Perhaps beneath that irresponsible charm there was a real love for her. Almost against her will, she returned his coaxing smile. "If you're really sure that Letty is safe . . . oh, all right, Desmond. You're a dreadful rogue, but what's done is done. I suppose that I will have to forgive you, and I hope that you have a vast success in Canada."

"All right, then," Desmond sighed in relief. "I couldn't bear to leave England thinking that you hated me. Look, you've had an exhausting day, and you have still have a long return journey ahead of you. Won't you sit down and have a

glass of wine with me, a bite to eat? Just to show me that
you've no hard feelings? Here's an excellent pigeon pie; I've
barely tasted it."

"Well, I've already ordered supper for me and Marie,
but . . . yes, I'll drink some wine with you." Dorinda sat
down, reaching for the glass of wine that Desmond had
poured for her. Her hand halted in midair as a voice from
behind her said, "Don't drink that, Miss Hayle."

Shalford, wearing a dust-covered, many-caped traveling
coat and a beaver hat, strode into the room, halting in front
of Desmond, who scrambled to his feet, his face expressing
angry alarm.

"I have an idea that the wine is drugged," said Shalford
coolly. He picked up the glass intended for Dorinda and held
it out to Desmond. "Here, Barry. You can disprove my
theory quickly enough. *You* drink it."

Dorinda stared at Desmond with a puzzled frown, as he
stepped away from the duke, placing his hands defensively
behind his back. Then, dismissing Desmond's behavior, she
braced her shoulders and turned back to the duke. "Good
evening, Your Grace. You've talked to Lady Lionel, I
presume."

"I have, indeed," replied Shalford calmly. "Julia tells me
that you came to her early this afternoon to say that my
future wife had eloped with this actor here."

"But I was mistaken," Dorinda exclaimed hastily. "Letty
didn't elope with Desmond—"

"I know she didn't. She has too much taste for that—or at
least some people might think so. She's gone off with young
Peregrine Lacey!"

"Perry and Letty? They've eloped?" stammered Dorinda.

Shalford nodded. "Incidentally," he continued in a con-
versational tone, "am I now to learn that Lady Letty was
actually a friend of this actor? I wasn't aware that they were
acquainted."

Feeling deflated, as if someone had stuck her with a pin, Dorinda sat down abruptly. She groped for words, saying, "I . . . they did meet several times. Well, Desmond knew *me*, of course. . . ."

Raising a grimly amused eyebrow at her floundering attempts to explain, Shalford turned his attention to Desmond who stood stiffly, his arms folded across his chest, his face a closed-in mask. "It was a fairly ingenious scheme, Barry, but it won't wash. Sit down, man. We're about to have a little talk to clear the air."

Slowly Desmond resumed his seat while Shalford crossed to the bell rope and pulled it vigorously. "A bottle of your best claret," he said to the inn servant who appeared a few moments later. Pulling up a chair beside Dorinda, he explained matter-of-factly, "It's been a thirsty journey and I need something to remove the dust from my throat, but I don't think that I care to sample any of Barry's brew. I was almost two hours behind you, Miss Hayle, and I've been springing my horses all the way to make up time. Job horses, of course. I only hope that I didn't cause my own team to break down on the first stage."

"How did you . . . I didn't think that Lady Lionel would—"

"A moment, Miss Hayle." Sipping the wine that the servant had just poured, Shalford nodded his dismissal and handed a glass to Dorinda. "You didn't think that my sister-in-law would betray your confidence? I can assure you, Julia had no intention of doing so. I have my niece Emily to thank for exposing Barry's conspiracy. Emily realized you were very upset when you came to see her mother today, you see. She became apprehensive, and after she saw you leave, she went straight to her mother. Without thinking, without the faintest idea of breaking your confidence, Julia asked Emily if she had observed any signs of unhappiness of late in Lady Letty. Now, Emily has always had an open face. She simply

cannot tell a successful lie. In this case, she had a guilty
conscience, and Julia knew immediately that Emily was
concealing something. Pressed, Emily admitted—and I
think she was really glad to have it out in the open, because
she had been sorely troubled—that Letty had confided in
her over a week ago that she and Perry Lacey had fallen in
love. It seems Letty was afraid she could never persuade her
grandmother to countenance the match—well, we know,
don't we, how very anxious Lady Torrington has been to see
Letty a duchess!"

Shooting Dorinda a cynical little smile, the duke continued: "So Letty and Perry decided that he would take her to
his parents' home at Eversleigh Court. Once the pair had
gotten safely away, Emily was to deliver a message to Lady
Torrington in which Letty threatened to elope with Lacey to
Gretna Green if her grandmother would not consent to her
marriage. Emily tried repeatedly to dissuade Letty from her
scheme, but Letty was convinced that she was doing nothing
wrong since she and Lacey had no real intention of eloping."

"That sounds like Letty," murmured Dorinda, shocked
but smiling despite herself.

"It does, doesn't it?" replied Shalford with an ironic twist
of his lips. "Well, then Julia recognized that something must
be very wrong, that you were involved in something sinister,
so she sent for me." He lifted an eyebrow. "I was listening at
the door for several minutes before I entered this room, Miss
Hayle. I heard Barry admit to luring you here by making
you believe he had eloped with Lady Letty. Didn't you
consider it quite a coincidence that Letty disappeared from
Torrington House this morning, thereby making it easy for
you to believe Barry's lie that he was eloping with her?"

"Why, yes, I did wonder about it, but Desmond merely
shrugged away the question."

"Well, he'll not shrug it off now." Shalford turned on
Desmond. "Barry, I want some answers from you."

"Answers to what, Your Grace? I've already admitted to Dorinda that I tried to trick her into going to Canada with me. But the plan failed."

"We know that much, Barry. We also know that you planned to drug Miss Hayle in the event she refused to accompany you to Canada. Didn't you suspect something, Miss Hayle, when Barry so easily accepted your decision to return to London? He was prepared for your refusal. It's just a guess, but I think tomorrow morning, after you had aroused from the drug, he planned to tell you that he had taken advantage of you during the night. With your 'virtue' gone, you would have had no choice but to go with him."

One look at Desmond's surly face convinced Dorinda that Shalford's guess was correct. Her face flaming, she jumped to her feet, advancing on Desmond with upraised arm. "Softly now," said Shalford with a grim smile as he caught Dorinda's arm and gently pushed her back into her chair. "What you really need, Miss Hayle, is a poker. You could use it to even better effect on Barry than you did on certain other gentlemen of our acquaintance. But you must curb your natural desire for vengeance. We need Barry whole and unharmed, at least until we get the rest of his story out of him."

Desmond stared at Shalford uneasily. "There isn't any rest of the story."

"My patience is wearing a little thin, Barry," said Shalford curtly. "If you don't tell us the truth voluntarily, I'll be forced to choke it out of you. Actually, at this point, I think I would enjoy a good mill. You do know that I've long been one of Gentleman Jackson's best pupils? Now, on the other hand," Shalford added casually, "if you were to make a clean breast of your villainy, I'd be prepared to give you twice the sum Mordaunt paid you."

"Sir Fabian!" gasped Dorinda.

"Yes, Miss Hayle. I fancy we'll find that Barry has been only a stalking-horse in this plot against you."

Hesitating for only a moment, Desmond threw up his arms and said, "Oh, very well, I'll tell you anything you want to know. I certainly don't owe Mordaunt anything. Double what he paid me, eh? That will cost you five thousand Yellow Boys, Your Grace."

"Five thousand guineas? That's coming it a bit too strong, surely?" The duke raised a skeptical eyebrow. "According to the *on-dit*, Mordaunt is fast aground. He couldn't have raised the wind for more than five hundred pounds, at most. Think again, Barry."

"You're a downy bird, Your Grace," said Desmond with a rueful smile. "Mordaunt did give me just five hundred pounds. I took a note for another five hundred. From what you say, I gather I'd have been hard put to collect on that note, although Sir Fabian did say he was coming into a fortune soon." Desmond shook his head. "The more I think about it, it was a stroke of luck that you and Dorinda caught up with me." Picking up the glass of wine he had poured for Dorinda, he was about to drain it when he paused, grinning crookedly, and crossed the room to pour the wine into the fireplace.

Dorinda watched him, her lips tightening in growing disgust. Then, turning her back on him when he returned to the table, she said to Shalford, "I'm very confused, Duke. What made you suspect Sir Fabian had anything to do with Desmond's scheme?"

"Because, after Emily's disclosure, I realized that Barry's attempt to lure you away on the very same day Peregrine Lacey eloped with Lady Letty was entirely too much of a coincidence," replied Shalford promptly. "And yet I could think of no connection between Lacey and Barry. As far as I knew, they were totally unacquainted with each other. Then I recalled that during the past week or so I had often seen

Lacey in Mordaunt's company. I'd wondered about this sudden friendship—the two seemingly had nothing in common—and it occurred to me that Mordaunt was the missing connection between Lacey and Barry. Here was a man who had a grudge against both of us, Miss Hayle. By wheedling his way into Lacey's confidence, he somehow arranged to settle the score with us in one brilliant stroke by having you abducted by Barry while at the same time he arranged for Peregrine Lacey to run off with my future fiancée. Do I have the general outline of the plot, Barry?"

Desmond gazed at Shalford, his expression one of reluctant admiration. "You're a devilish knowing cove, Your Grace. You could have knocked me over with a feather a week or so ago when Sir Fabian sought me out at Covent Garden—as you know, I'm certainly not in the same social class as the Prince Regent's equerry, and besides, he wasn't best pleased with me the last time we met. Remember, Dorinda? I'd arranged for him to have a friendly chat with my new singer-actress, and then she attacked him with a poker!"

Exchanging a quick look with Shalford, Dorinda bit her lip. The duke said impatiently, "Spare us your reminiscences, Barry, and get on with your story."

"Well, to my surprise, Sir Fabian invited me to his lodgings," began Desmond. "We cracked a bottle or two, and chatted about this and that, and it soon become apparent he was aware that Dorinda Hayle and Rachel Conroy were the same person. He offered to pay me for any information I could give him about you, Dorinda." Desmond spread his hands in a shamefaced gesture. "I didn't like to peach on you, my girl, but . . . well, he already knew that you were the actress Rachel Conroy, didn't he? I didn't see how I could do you much more harm by telling him what he wanted to know—and I was pinched for the needful. I haven't told you, Dorinda, but the fact is, my provincial touring com-

pany has fallen on hard times. The bailiff in Margate has
seized all the company costumes, scenery, and musical
instruments against nonpayment of debts. I couldn't leave
all my players in the lurch, could I?"

"In other circumstances my heart might bleed for your
misfortunes," snapped the duke. "Please continue."

"In a moment . . . Dorinda, won't you try to understand
my position? I do love you, after all, and I really did think
you and I could be happy, starting all over in a new country. . . . Oh, very well," he said sullenly as he noted the
duke's quelling glance, "I'll get on with it. I told Sir Fabian
everything I knew about you, Dorinda. Your relationship to
Lady Torrington through her son, the facts of your mother's
stage career, the name of the village where Lady Roger
lives—that sort of thing. Even—this was well into the evening, after the third bottle or so of port—even a story about
your mother that I'd completely forgotten, something my
father told me years ago when he was in his cups, about how
Charlotte—Lady Roger—had once had a romance with a
real swell, a peer's son, no less. It seems this man actually
wanted to marry Charlotte, but then his father got wind of
the affair, whisked the swell away to make a tour of the
continent or some such, and paid Charlotte a handsome sum
for her heartbreak. According to my father, Charlotte—
sorry, Lady Roger—never saw the swell again. She only
discovered after he was gone that she was with child."
Desmond looked inquiringly at Dorinda. "But I suppose you
know the story better than I do. The swell must have been
your father."

"Where did Mr. Barry get such a story?" asked Dorinda
blankly. "My father was one of Mama's fellow actors." She
shook her head. "Even if the story *were* true, why would it
interest Sir Fabian? For that matter, why has he been
prying into my past history at all?"

"Obviously he hasn't given up hope of somehow paying

you back for humiliating him in Brighton," said the duke quietly. "He was probably just nosing about, trying to ferret out any information that he might use to discredit you."

"But how could he think this story about my father being a peer's son rather than an actor would do me any harm? Lady Torrington already knows that I'm illegitimate. And, Duke, I thought you had silenced Sir Fabian, seen to it that he couldn't spread any gossip about me."

"I stopped him from acting openly against you, yes. Apparently he thought his participation in this present plot would never come to light. What I think happened is this: Mordaunt cultivated Peregrine Lacey, knowing that the youngster was an old friend of Letty's and perhaps hoping merely to pick up some morsel of information he could use against you, Miss Hayle, as he had already done in the case of Mr. Barry. Discovering that Perry and Letty had fallen in love, he suddenly saw how to kill two birds with one stone. And what is more, he could do it anonymously. In the guise of an older, more experienced friend, he planted the idea of eloping in Lacey's mind. He remained in Perry's confidence and thus was informed of the date of the elopement, which he passed on to Barry who could then use Letty's absence from Torrington House as a cover to persuade you, Miss Hayle, that he had gone off with Lady Letty. Does that cover the facts pretty well, Barry?"

"Very well indeed, sir," replied Desmond promptly. A flicker of malicious amusement crossed his face. "Lord, I'd give a pound or two to see Mordaunt's face when he realizes that you're safely back in London, Dorinda. I didn't like that fellow or his schemes above half."

"But your dislike didn't prevent you from accepting Sir Fabian's money, did it?" said Dorinda, curling her lip.

"But Dorinda, I've tried to tell you——" began Desmond. However, Shalford cut him off, saying, "Save your breath, Barry. Miss Hayle is too intelligent to be taken in by you again." As Desmond's face burned a deep red, Shalford added casually, "Did your father by any chance mention the name of the titled gentleman who he thought was Miss Hayle's father?"

"That's what Mordaunt wanted to know. I can't imagine why. But I couldn't remember the name, except that it sounded like grass, or grasshopper, although that don't sound likely." Desmond rose. "Well, Your Grace, I don't think that I can tell you anything more. So if you'll just hand over the rhino, I'll retire gracefully to the wings." He smiled a little sadly. "I daresay you could call this a farewell benefit performance, eh? And a very well-paid one, too."

"I don't have two thousand pounds with me, Barry. I can have it sent to Covent Garden or to your rooms in London. Or, if you're determined to go to Canada, I'll send the money on to you care of the receiving office in Bristol."

"Make it Bristol. I might as well go to Canada. I'm certainly not insane enough to return to London. Mordaunt will want my hide when he finds out that I've taken his blunt and haven't delivered the goods," replied Desmond frankly. Picking up his hat and his greatcoat, he walked to the door, lingering on the threshold to say, "Good-bye, Dorinda. I doubt that we'll ever meet again. No hard feelings? I swear I meant you no real harm. And who's to say that you wouldn't have loved Canada!"

Dorinda looked at Desmond resignedly. A jaunty smile was already erasing his downcast expression. She shook her head. "Good-bye, Desmond."

After he had left, Shalford said, "Sit down and try to relax a bit, Miss Hayle. I'm off to order rooms for us and a good dinner, which I think both of us sorely need. I'll also arrange to have Julia's chambermaid sent back to London by the first stagecoach tomorrow morning. I'll drive you back in my curricle."

"Oh, but I can't stay here until morning. I must return to London immediately. Lady Torrington—"

"It would mean traveling all night," warned Shalford. "You're already exhausted. And have you forgotten? Unless Barry was lying, Lady Torrington has already received his note saying that you and he were eloping."

Dorinda's hands flew to her face. "I had forgotten," she said almost inaudibly. Then, throwing her shoulders back, she exclaimed, "All the more reason to go back, to put Lady Torrington straight about me. And about Letty, too," she added in alarm. "After receiving Desmond's letter, Lady Torrington won't know what to think about Letty's absence."

"She does now. I asked my sister-in-law to tell Lady Torrington about Letty's elopement. I thought that the dowager ought to know about the situation as soon as possible since, as Letty's guardian, she's the only person who can deal with it. And I'm sure that Lady Torrington will guess from Julia's explanation that you haven't really eloped with Barry. So you see, there's no pressing need for you to return to London tonight. I strongly advise a meal and a good night's rest."

Dorinda drooped, feeling suddenly very tired and at least ten years older than she had been that morning. "Yes, I know you're right. There's no point in returning tonight," she muttered. "In fact, I don't relish the thought of an interview with Lady Torrington at *any* time. She's not going to like anything that's happened today."

"That, Miss Hayle, is a masterpiece of understatement," observed the duke cynically.

Chapter XII

It was quite an excellent supper—a beefsteak, a pigeon pie, asparagus, some cherry tarts—but Dorinda, lost in her bittersweet thoughts, consumed the meal without really tasting what she was eating. Across the table, Shalford was silent too, though occasionally she would glance up to find him looking at her.

Finally, over a post-dinner glass of port, Shalford asked abruptly, "Miss Hayle, why didn't you tell me that Lady Letitia didn't want to marry me?"

"I wasn't at all sure that she didn't want to marry you," exclaimed Dorinda. "She seemed shy of you, unready for marriage just at this time perhaps, especially to the second peer of the realm. . . ."

"So she didn't appear to you to be troubled or unhappy?"

"Well . . . not until the very end, at least. I certainly had no idea that she was in love with Perry!" Dorinda turned a troubled gaze on Shalford. "I really don't think that she *is* in love with Perry. If you and Lady Torrington were to leave

Letty to herself for a while, not pressuring her, allowing her to make up her own mind, she might well discover that it's you she wants to marry after all. Why, she and Perry have always been just good friends, childhood playmates!"

"Oh, I think a trifle more than childhood playmates," said Shalford dryly. His face turned thoughtful, and he spoke in a low voice, almost as if he had forgotten Dorinda's presence. "You know, I hadn't really planned to marry at all. Then my nephew died, and I knew that I had to provide for the succession. Still, I wasn't interested in tying myself for life to any of the girls I saw coming out season after season. They were all the same, shallow and insipid, clothes- and party-mad—"

"And of course you preferred looser, earthier, unconventional types like Cassandra Bell!" To her horror, Dorinda realized that she had been speaking aloud, and her face flamed crimson.

"So it *was* you, that afternoon in the Covent Garden Green Room," exclaimed Shalford, breaking into a laugh. "I wondered a bit when I first caught sight of you, a distressed gentlewoman, so out of place in that crowd of actors. There was something about the way you walked, the way you held your head, that seemed familiar. But then, outside the theatre, when I heard that atrocious Cockney voice— Oh, it was a marvelous disguise, Miss Hayle!"

His amusement fading, Shalford went on, "Well, you're correct, of course. Cassandra Bell and her like do have a certain attraction for me, but obviously they are not marriageable material. I was rather looking for a girl of quality who would be a little out of the way, have a bit of spice in her personality, and the brains and character to keep me interested for the rest of our life together. I thought last winter that I had found such a girl in Lady Letty. What an enchanting, vibrant creature she seemed, without a hint of insipidity. But when I met her in town during the season, most of that lovely vivacity was missing. She often seemed, Heaven help me, like a schoolgirl—a rather shy one just released from the schoolroom. When I talked to her I sometimes felt more like an uncle than a suitor!"

"But you *are* much older than Letty," said Dorinda defensively. "And she *is* just out of the schoolroom. I've been trying to tell you, she was unsure of herself with you, afraid that she couldn't live up to the responsibilities of her new position."

Shalford looked at Dorinda thoughtfully. "But in conversation with other people, especially with Peregrine Lacey, she appeared to be the lively refreshing girl I had met originally. It was just with me that there seemed to be this restraint." He paused. "Would you have allowed the situation to go on, with Lady Letty growing more and more unhappy, if she hadn't seized the initiative herself and gone off with Perry Lacey?"

"I don't know," replied Dorinda miserably. "I knew that you adored her and it would break your heart if she didn't marry you, and I couldn't bear the thought of your being hurt." Dorinda stopped abruptly.

Shalford said quietly, "I thought I did care deeply for Lady Letty."

Dorinda raised her head quickly, sitting very still as he continued.

"I believed that I was in love with Letty," said Shalford, "until the morning I stormed into Torrington House, breathing fire at my discovery that you were the same enticing actress I had tried to seduce in Brighton. I was so angry with you that I could cheerfully have strangled you. Instead, of course, I made love to you, only to have you repulse me again. Later that same day I realized I had been courting the wrong woman. I understood the reason for the warm glow I felt in Letty's company; you were always there too—

the mature, fascinating, and entrancingly lovely woman I must have been looking for all my life!"

Dorinda drew a startled breath. "You were out of your mind!"

"No, but I was certainly in a depressed state of mind," replied Shalford with an odd smile. "I knew there was no way I could cry off from the engagement, even though it wasn't yet official. Lady Torrington expected me to offer for Letty. I thought Letty herself expected me to do so. I'm ashamed to admit that I was overjoyed when Letty scandalously ran off with Perry Lacey. I was off the hook!" He reached across the table for Dorinda's hand. "My dearest darling, it's you I want to marry. Is there any chance that you might come to love me too?"

"I think I've loved you from the first moment we met, even when you were trying to turn me into one of your doxies," Dorinda blurted, wondering in some detached portion of her mind how she had managed to keep her true feelings from herself for so long.

Rising so quickly that his chair crashed to the floor behind him, Shalford pulled Dorinda to her feet and clasped her in his arms. For a few sensuously enchanted moments, she surrendered herself to the warmth of his seeking lips, to the racing excitement of feeling his erratically thudding heart against her own. Then, her breath coming in short, shallow bursts, she managed to pull herself away. "We must stop this. It's madness. How could you even think of marrying someone with my background? You said it yourself. Cassandra Bell and her like attract you, but they aren't 'marriageable material.' Well, I'm another Cassandra Bell."

Reaching out a long arm, Shalford seized Dorinda by the shoulder. "You are not. You're nothing like her," he protested hotly. "You're not a professional actress, not a compliant creature of the moment. You're a sensitive, cultured, utterly wonderful lady of quality."

"Justin . . ." Dorinda paused a moment, wistfully savoring her first use of his given name. "Justin, I may not be a professional actress, but my mother certainly was—and I *am* illegitimate. Society would never accept me as your wife. Look at my stepfather. From the day Lord Roger married my mother, Lady Torrington never again accepted him as her son."

"Perhaps Lady Torrington is more insecure about her social position than I am. The Dukedom of Shalford, after all, was created in 1485," retorted the duke with a flash of his old haughtiness. He put a reassuring arm around Dorinda. "In any event, I don't care what people say of me, thought I wouldn't want to see *you* unhappy, or to know that you felt you were not accepted. But my darling, I really don't think the problem is as acute as you imagine. Your mother *is* Lady Roger Wingate, and her past life must be largely forgotten by now, if indeed many people ever heard of it. If she's like you, she must be a charming person, well able to hold her own when she comes to visit us. After we're married, if there are any rumors, they will circulate behind our backs. Nobody will dare to mention anything embarrassing to our faces, I promise you." Shalford's expression turned suddenly grim.

Dorinda surveyed him with an odd, tender little smile. "We needn't make any decision right now," she said, going to him and putting her arms around his neck while she cuddled her head against his chest. "Let's just enjoy this moment of happiness while we can," she murmured.

Disengaging himself from her embrace, Shalford held her at arm's length. "Don't imagine that I'll give you up," he scowled. "You'll marry me if I have to drag you by the hair to Gretna Green. But you're tired now. Go get a good night's sleep, and we'll talk about all this tomorrow."

The long, grueling day had taken its toll and the bed in her chamber was very comfortable, but Dorinda found it difficult to fall asleep. Her thoughts veered from ecstasy to despair, from soaring joy in her new-found love to the bleak realization that the problems caused by their disparity of station would inevitably put an intolerable strain on a marriage between her and Justin. His detached, coolly logical mind would surely come to the same conclusion, she reflected the next morning as she went down the stairs to join him for breakfast, once he had recovered from the first throes of this disturbing new passion. She paused at the door of the dining parlor. But today is mine, she thought with sudden fierce joy. For just this one day, until they arrived back in London, she could pretend that this lovely, aching happiness would last forever.

In the dining parlor, Justin rose at her entrance, his aloof features transformed by a radiant, boyish smile. "There you are, my darling. I was getting so impatient to see you that I was about to come up and get you. Come have some coffee. But first. . . ." He drew her closely into his arms, pressing his mouth to hers in a long, throbbing kiss.

If Dorinda had marveled at the speed and ease of travel in a chaise and four, she had to revise her ideas of luxury as a passenger in Shalford's curricle. At each stop, the needs of lesser and more humble travelers were totally ignored when the duke drove into the courtyard; hostlers changed his teams with a smoothness and dispatch that she would have thought impossible, while the landlord hovered obsequiously nearby with several servants who awaited the least command from the ducal lips.

The little towns rolled by in reverse: Newbury, Thatcham, Reading, Twyford, Maidenhead. They had left Hungerford shortly before nine, and as the curricle ate up the miles, Dorinda estimated that they would arrive in London in some ten hours. But where the westbound journey from London the day before had dragged interminably, now Dorinda found to her dismay that the minutes and the hours were flashing by relentlessly. She and Justin did not say very much. He concentrated his keen eyes and powerfully capable hands on his driving. Then, too, the presence of his tiger on the perch behind them was inhibiting. But occasionally Dorinda would burrow closer to Justin, to feel the comforting sinewy strength of his body next to hers; then he would turn briefly and favor her with one of the warmly tender smiles with which she was growing familiar.

All too soon, as the bright summer day faded into late afternoon, they passed through Hyde Park Corner and turned into Piccadilly and then into Berkeley Square. The tiger leaped nimbly down to hold the horses and Justin lifted his arms to help Dorinda from the curricle. Giving him her hand, she attempted a lightness that she did not feel: "I'll write, to tell you how Lady Torrington receives me. But don't be surprised if my letter comes from Eastfield! I daresay that I won't be able to stay in Torrington House long enough to write a letter to you, not once the dowager dresses me down and dismisses me!"

Justin shook his head. "There will be no dressing down, Dorinda. I'm coming in with you."

"I can't let you do that. Letty was my responsibility. Her grandmother has a right to demand a reckoning from me."

"Lady Letty may not be my responsibility, but you are, dearest," replied the duke firmly. "And I'm not going to let Lady Torrington browbeat you."

"Well, if you insist . . ." said Dorinda weakly.

"I do," said Justin, giving her his arm as they passed under the graceful wrought-iron arch and up the entrance steps.

"Good afternoon, Frith. Is Lady Torrington in?" asked Dorinda when the butler answered the door.

"Yes indeed, Miss Hayle. I trust your sick friend is better? Good afternoon, Your Grace. Her ladyship is in the drawing room." Frith's normally inscrutable face wore an oddly bemused expression that caught Dorinda's attention and caused her to pause momentarily, her brow furrowed. "I wonder what has upset Frith," she murmured, as she walked with Shalford up the stairs to the drawing room. "Usually he shows as much feeling as the Great Sphinx. Do you suppose that he's found out about Letty? . . ."

She halted, transfixed, on the threshold of the drawing room. Lady Torrington, her face a mask of baffled outrage, sat staring at Charlotte Wingate. Posed gracefully on the settee, Charlotte was wearing a simple black pelisse and a bonnet of first mourning. The effect she created was one of elegance.

"Mama, what on earth are you doing here?" cried Dorinda.

Beaming, Charlotte held out her welcoming arms. "Dearest, you've returned. I've only just arrived, and I was so disappointed not to find you here. Something has been worrying me, you see—oh, just a trifle—and I felt that I had to talk to you. You know, I haven't been in London in almost twenty years, and I find it so changed."

"We can talk later, Mama," said Dorinda gently, bending down to kiss her. "I'd like to present to you the Duke of Shalford. Your Grace, this is my mother, Lady Roger Wingate." Dorinda shot a glance at Lady Torrington, whose forbidding features indicated clearly that making known her daughter-in-law to the duke was only slightly less catastrophic than exposing him to the Black Death.

Looking pleased as she always did at receiving male attention, Charlotte smiled prettily at the duke as he bowed over her hand. "Dorinda wrote to tell me how kind you've been, Your Grace. Riding lessons, fancy that! And a horse!"

Looking at her mother's beguiling smile, listening to her beautifully modulated voice, Dorinda wondered fleetingly if Lady Torrington's cruelly dismissive attitude toward her son's wife might have been different if she had ever met Charlotte in the flesh.

Bracing herself, Dorinda turned to the dowager. "I'm very sorry about Letty."

"So, you've come back, Miss Hayle," said Lady Torrington at her most overpowering. "As I suspected, you had far too much sense to elope with an actor—and too much sad family precedence also, I might add." To Shalford, she said, "An unhappy day, Duke. I scarcely know what to say to you. This morning I received an express from Lady Lacey, informing me that she had asked Letty to stay with her at Eversleigh Court. So now we know for certain that Letty hasn't actually eloped with that young villain, Peregrine Lacey, and with just a touch of good fortune we may hope to avoid an open scandal with my chit of a granddaughter. I presume that there is no point in asking you if you can forgive the girl."

"There's nothing to forgive, Lady Torrington. But I think there's no doubt that Lady Letty and I don't suit."

The dowager sighed heavily. "I thought as much. It's a very great pity." She shrugged. "Well, there's nothing to be done. I suppose I shall be obliged in the end to allow Letty and Peregrine to marry. But what an imprudent match! He a younger son with no prospects at all, as likely as not to be sent to the Peninsula and blown to smithereens!"

"I can't guarantee Perry's safety with the Duke of Wellington in the Peninsula, of course," commented Shalford mildly, "but his ancestry and family are impeccable, and surely Lady Letty has a large enough fortune for both of them. Actually, it might even be an ideal match. They both love country life, they're both horse mad, and I suspect that Lady Letty might just enjoy being a camp follower in Portugal!"

"That's scarcely a reassuring prospect," replied the dowager dryly. She sighed again, remarking to Dorinda, "I know that I shouldn't beat a dead horse, Miss Hayle, but I can't but feel you might have tried harder to ward off the very catastrophe that I hired you to prevent."

Shalford stepped up to Dorinda, taking her hand protectively. "I can't allow you to reproach Dorinda, Lady Torrington. She went far beyond the demands of duty in attempting to prevent what she thought to be Lady Letty's elopement. As a matter of fact, she was in serious danger of being abducted herself. And I think I should also tell you that Dorinda and I are betrothed."

The dowager's complexion turned an alarming shade of dark red as she thundered, "You must be mad even to think of such a marriage, Duke. Do you realize that this girl, though technically she is my stepgranddaughter, is actually the daughter of a notorious actress, and illegitimate to boot?"

"I know everything there is to know about Dorinda," retorted Shalford, his fury barely controlled, and Dorinda murmured forlornly, "Oh, Justin, why did you tell her about us?"

Then Charlotte, quite as if she had not heard the dowager's blast, remarked in pleased, interested tones, "Well, darling, marrying a duke, are you? If I had known your good news, I shouldn't have been so worried, and I needn't have come chasing after you to London. His Grace will take very good care of you, I'm sure, even if that other man tries to make mischief for you."

"What man, Mama?" asked Dorinda in surprise, and Justin's face assumed a thoughtful, intent look.

Charlotte sounded faintly apologetic. "Well, dearest, I know we agreed that I wasn't to talk about your employment with Lady Torrington. I understood perfectly that she didn't like my connection to the stage to be known. But last week this very elegant gentleman came to Eastfield to see me. He said he was Sir Fabian Mordaunt, equerry to the

Prince Regent himself, and a London friend of yours. Naturally, I invited him to tea. He was such a warm, sympathetic person, and I don't know how it was exactly—perhaps I've been a little lonely with you so far away, dearest—but soon I found myself chattering away about you, and our relationship to Lady Torrington, and Lord Roger's death, and my experience on the stage, and even about—" Charlotte stopped short.

"Well, I won't go into it," she resumed a moment later, "but I told Sir Fabian something that seemed to make him quite angry—I can't imagine why—and he left the house almost immediately. So then I got to worrying. Could he be plotting to do you some harm? I couldn't rest until I had warned you, so I begged dear kind Mrs. Vane for the use of the vicarage carriage to take me into Brighton, and there I caught the next available stagecoach to London. I'm so very sorry, my darling. I really didn't mean to be such a gabblemonger."

Feeling a sudden murderous urge to throttle Sir Fabian, Dorinda sat down beside Charlotte on the settee and put a comforting arm around her shoulders. "Don't worry anymore, Mama. That dreadful man can't do anything to hurt me now."

"No, dismiss Mordaunt from your mind, Lady Roger. I think that we've brought him to a stand," said the duke.

The dowager lifted a bewildered eyebrow. "What's this about Sir Fabian Mordaunt? What possible connection can he have with you, Miss Hayle?"

"He schemed to have Dorinda abducted, and I'm almost certain he put the idea of eloping with Letty into Peregrine Lacey's head," said Shalford bluntly. "I'll tell you about it later, if you really want to know the shoddy details. But for now . . . please don't think that I'm being merely inquisitive, Lady Roger, but might I ask you just what it was that you told Mordaunt that made him so angry? Was it about Dorinda's father?"

Charlotte's pretty color vanished. She clutched at Dorinda's hand, faltering, "What a strange question, Your Grace."

"Lady Roger, I realize that this is very embarrassing to you, but it's very important that you answer the question. Did you tell Mordaunt that Dorinda's father was named Mossley? And did you also tell Mordaunt that you had married this Mossley?"

"Mossley!" exclaimed Lady Torrington, thunderstruck.

"Mama, I don't understand," said Dorinda blankly. "Were you and my father actually married?"

Fumbling in her reticule, Charlotte brought out a wisp of linen and dabbed at the tears coursing down her cheeks. "Dorinda, darling, I don't like to talk about it . . . well, you know how sensitive you've always been about your birth. I remember so well how crushed you felt when that unkind lady, the mother of your classmate at the academy, changed her mind about inviting you to her home when she discovered that . . . that my union with your father was, well, irregular."

The dowager's puzzled expression and Justin's air of controlled expectancy caused Dorinda to say quietly, "I think perhaps you'd better tell me all about it, Mama. Desmond Barry—you remember the actor who called on us in Brighton last winter—once told me that my father wasn't an actor, but rather a peer's son who actually proposed marriage to you."

"Oh!" gasped Charlotte. "How did Mr. Barry know? . . ." For several moments she sat with her eyes downcast, her fingers nervously shredding her handkerchief, until finally she looked up at Dorinda with a wan smile. "Since you already know that much—yes, Hector *did* want to marry me. In fact, we skipped up to Gretna Green where the tollkeeper performed the ceremony right in the tollhouse. Of course, we *could* have been married by the blacksmith, can you fancy that? Because in Scotland, all you need do to marry is to make a declaration before witnesses." Charlotte shook her head, obviously still fascinated by the vagaries of Scottish law.

Dorinda's face revealed her bewilderment. "But Mama, why didn't you ever tell me that you and Papa were married?"

Taking Dorinda's hand, Charlotte said sadly, "Because we really weren't, dearest. Less than a month after we returned from Scotland, Hector's Papa caught up with us in York, where I was playing. He threatened to cut Hector off without a penny, and to disinherit him from everything that wasn't entailed unless Hector left me immediately and sued to have the 'marriage' annulled. Poor Hector had to give in. He hadn't a feather to fly with, and the Lord knows, *I* wasn't earning very much. Besides, I think by this time Hector was beginning to have second thoughts about marrying me. So he went away, and his father was really quite generous to me, I must admit that. But it wasn't until after Hector had gone that I discovered I was with child. If I'd known sooner, I think I would have fought to delay the annullment until after you were born, dearest, so that you could have been born legitimate. But . . ." Charlotte shrugged in defeat.

"Lady Roger, I think that Dorinda *is* legitimate," Shalford intervened quietly. "She was certainly 'lawfully begotten,' even though the union was later dissolved."

"Shalford, are you saying what I think you're saying?" demanded Lady Torrington incredulously.

"I am. I believe that Dorinda is the rightful 'lost heiress' of Hector Mossley, that she is Baroness Caldecott in her own right, rather than Miss Adelaide Ware whom Sir Fabian Mordaunt has been courting these many weeks. When Mordaunt accidentally discovered from Desmond

Barry that Dorinda might be Mossley's daughter, he went down to Brighton to ferret out the truth from Lady Roger. One is almost tempted to feel sorry for the man. His engagement to Miss Ware is all but official, and then he learns that Dorinda may well inherit the money and the title. Since Dorinda despises him, he knows that he has no chance with her, so he pays Desmond Barry to abduct her to Canada where there is no possibility that she will ever learn of her heritage."

"Sir Fabian had Miss Hayle abducted because she despised him? Shalford, you're making very little sense," complained the dowager.

Briefly, Shalford acquainted both Lady Torrington and Charlotte with the details of Sir Fabian's plot, including in his account the story of Dorinda's encounter with the equerry during her short stage career—which caused the dowager to turn faintly purple—and the tie-in with Letty's elopement with Peregrine Lacey.

"I can understand why you suspected Sir Fabian's hand in both Miss Hayle's abduction and Letty's elopement," said Lady Torrington when Shalford had finished. "But I don't quite see how you made the connection between Miss Hayle and Hector Mossley."

"I just thought Mordaunt's revenge on Dorinda was a bit excessive," explained Shalford, adding with a teasing smile, "after all, her only offense was to hit him with a poker! Then I had a sort of inspiration when Barry revealed that he'd told Mordaunt the old story about Dorinda's father, and I found myself asking Barry if he had also told Mordaunt the name of Dorinda's putative noble parent. Do you remember what he said, my love?"

Dorinda, who had been sitting in dazed bewilderment for the past several minutes, said slowly, "Desmond thought my father's name was grasshopper." She broke into a nervous giggle as Shalford exclaimed triumphantly, "Exactly so! My mind instantly made the leap between grass and moss, and there the truth stood revealed: Dorinda was Hector Mossley's daughter; not only that, she was Mossley's *legitimate* daughter, or why else would she be a threat to Mordaunt's marriage plans?"

"It's like something out of one of those dreadful novels that Letty is always reading," marveled Lady Torrington. "To think that Fabian Mordaunt has turned out to be such an unmitigated villain. But Shalford," she added sharply, "you can't bring him to book for this without causing enormous scandal in the Prince Regent's circle. I can assure you that His Royal Highness wouldn't like it above half."

"No, I quite agree, much as I would prefer otherwise," replied the duke reluctantly.

"It will be punishment enough for Sir Fabian to lose his heiress," continued Lady Torrington. "And speaking of heiresses, I've definitely decided to allow Letty to marry Peregrine Lacey, if I am satisfied that they really care for each other. At least, with Letty safely married, I shan't have these constant worries about her bursting out in some sort of unseemly behavior!" She rose to pull vigorously at the bell rope, and turned to Charlotte, saying, "We must have a room prepared for you at once, Lady Roger. You must be very fatigued after your long journey from Brighton."

"Indeed, I am tired, Lady Torrington. I would like to rest," Charlotte replied simply. She left the drawing room shortly afterward with the dowager, who paused at the door to say, "Naturally, you'll stay to dinner, Shalford. We have so many plans to make for the wedding, or I should say the two weddings, Letty's and Dorinda's."

Dorinda gaped. "I must be dreaming," she said unbelievingly. "Mama a guest in this house? Lady Torrington to help plan my wedding?"

"My darling peagoose, the dowager sees your mama differently now that Lady Roger is the widow of *two* titled men, in a manner of speaking, of course. Your mama's marriage to your papa was annulled, but since he never remarried, I presume that she has as much right to be his widow as anybody! And now that Lady Letty isn't going to become the Duchess of Shalford, Lady Torrington has no objection to her stepgranddaughter, the Baroness Caldecott, assuming that position!"

A shadow crossed Dorinda's face, and she clenched her hands tightly together as she said, "Justin, I can't quite grasp this idea of being a baroness. Miss Ware has already succeeded to the title. Wouldn't it be necessary to dispute her claim? That could result in so much gossip and speculation. Mama's entire life would be on public display. And there's Miss Ware herself. She's really a very nice woman. I should dislike very much causing her pain or embarrassment."

Shalford put his arm around Dorinda. "My darling, we'll do just as you like," he assured her quietly. "It's probably true that the Crown Office has already terminated the title on Miss Ware. Disputing her claim would undoubtedly result in considerable gossip, and there's not much about your life or Lady Roger's that would remain private. But just say the word, and I'll gladly fight your claim for you."

Dorinda turned away from him. "I don't know what I should do," she said wretchedly. "I've no great desire to be a baroness, but last night at Hungerford I decided that I couldn't marry you with this stain on my birth. So now that I have this opportunity to be declared legitimate, I'm tempted to let you fight my case for me, Justin. Still, even if we won, even if I became the Baroness Caldecott, how could I marry you under such a cloud of scandal and publicity? No matter that Lady Torrington has finally accepted Mama. I'm very sure that the daughter of a professional actress should not become the next Duchess of Shalford."

Snatching Dorinda into his arms, Shalford declared vehemently, "It doesn't matter a whit to me if you have a title or not, and if society chooses to cut me because my wife's mother was an actress, so be it. Better that than to live desolate for what years remain to me because I've lost the only woman I will ever love. I'd rather like to see you a baroness for your own self-esteem, but for myself, I really don't care. I'd want to marry you, my foolish, adorable Dorinda, if you were a chimney sweep's daughter!"

Sighing, Dorinda wound her arms around the duke's neck. "I seem to have mislaid my pride and my willpower and my common sense," she murmured. "And I don't miss them at all. All I can think of is how happy I am to be in your arms."